"My bedroom is upstairs."

"And?"

"It's where I keep my Beretta."

"Say no more."

He scooped her into his arms and cradled her against his chest. Her good arm was closest to his body, and she slipped her hand up and around his neck. Her intention had been to make it easier to carry her. The effect was different—warm, sensual and intimate.

Emily had known Connor for years, which meant plenty of hugs and casual physical contact. Once or twice, they'd danced together. Other than the few kisses they'd shared, nothing had felt as extraordinary and personal as this moment. It seemed like they existed in a bubble that was their own special world.

Two layers of fabric separated them: her velour sweatshirt and his black V-neck cashmere sweater. And yet their touch started a friction that thrilled her. Was it possible for her to hear his heartbeat or was she imagining the steady, strong thump? She was utterly, totally, happily aware of him as a man.

THE GIRL WHO WOULDN'T STAY DEAD

USA TODAY Bestselling Author

CASSIE MILES

To Annie Underwood Perry and the latest addition to her family.
And, as always, to Rick.

Recycling programs
for this product may
not exist in your area.

ISBN-13: 978-1-335-52671-7

The Girl Who Wouldn't Stay Dead

Copyright © 2018 by Kay Bergstrom

Printed in U.S.A.

www.Harlequin.com

Cassie Miles, a *USA TODAY* bestselling author, lives in Colorado. After raising two daughters and cooking tons of macaroni and cheese for her family, Cassie is trying to be more adventurous in her culinary efforts. She's discovered that almost anything tastes better with wine. When she's not plotting Harlequin Intrigue books, Cassie likes to hang out at the Denver Botanic Gardens near her high-rise home.

Books by Cassie Miles

Harlequin Intrigue

Mountain Midwife
Sovereign Sheriff
Baby Battalion
Unforgettable
Midwife Cover
Mommy Midwife
Montana Midwife
Hostage Midwife
Mountain Heiress
Snowed In
Snow Blind
Mountain Retreat
Colorado Wildfire
Mountain Bodyguard
Mountain Shelter
Mountain Blizzard
Frozen Memories
The Girl Who Wouldn't Stay Dead

Visit the Author Profile page at Harlequin.com.

CAST OF CHARACTERS

Emily Benton-Riggs—She escaped a rough childhood and a bad marriage. Will she survive a murderer who comes after her again and again?

Connor Gallagher—For years, he's been Emily's lawyer and best friend. He hopes their relationship will evolve into something more.

Jamison Riggs—Emily divorced the Wall Street broker over a year ago. He died recently under mysterious circumstances.

Glenda Riggs—The matriarch of the wealthy, powerful family based in Aspen, Colorado.

Patricia Riggs—Jamison's cousin is a sharp businesswoman who keeps the family enterprises running smoothly.

Phillip Riggs—Patricia's ski-bum brother lives in the house that Emily recently inherited from her deceased ex-husband.

Dr. Eric Thorson—The ER doctor at a clinic in Aspen has a specialty in virology. He is engaged to Patricia.

Kate Sylvester—Jamison's fiery lover and partner at the brokerage firm has a talent for breaking up marriages.

Deputy Rafe Sandoval—The Pitkin County officer is the first to suspect murder.

SAC Jaiden Wellborn—The well-dressed FBI agent who specializes in white-collar crime started his investigation with Jamison's death.

Robert O'Brien—A detective hired by Connor to follow up on the investigation.

TJ Beverly—She's a former marine who is hired as a bodyguard by Connor.

Chapter One

She had to wake up. Someone was trying to kill her.

Her eyelids snapped open. Her vision was blurred. Every part of her body hurt.

Emily Benton-Riggs inhaled a sharp gasp. The chilly night air pierced her lungs like a knife between the ribs. Slowly, she exhaled, then drew a breath again and tried to focus. She was still in the car but not sitting upright. Her little Hyundai had flipped, rolled and smacked into the granite side of a mountain at least twice on the way down, maybe more. The car had landed on the driver's side.

Likewise, her brain was jumbled. Nothing was clear.

Even in her dazed state, she was glad to be alive—grateful and also a little bit surprised. The past few years of her life had moments of such flat-out misery that she'd come to expect the worst. And yet, recently, things seemed to be turning around. She liked her rented bungalow in Denver, and her work was satisfying. Plus, she'd just learned that she might be a very wealthy woman. *I can't give up.* It'd take more than crashing through the guardrail on a narrow mountain road near Aspen and plummeting down a sheer cliff to kill her.

Her forehead felt damp. When she pushed her bangs back and touched the wet spot above her hairline, her pain shot into high gear. Every twitch, every movement set off a fresh agony. Her hand came away bloody.

Her long-dead mother—an angry woman who didn't believe in luck or spontaneous adventure or love, especially not love—burst into her imagination. Her mom, with her wild, platinum hair and her clothes askew, took a swig from her vodka bottle and grumbled in harsh words only Emily could hear, "You don't deserve that vast fortune. That's why you're dead."

"But I'm not," Emily protested aloud. "And I deserve this inheritance. I loved Jamison. I did everything I could to stay married to him. It's not my fault that he slept with…practically everybody."

Her voice trailed off. She never wanted to relive the humiliating final chapter of her marriage. It was over.

"You failed," her mother said with a sneer.

"Go away. I'm not going to argue with a ghost."

"You'll be joining me soon enough." Unearthly, eerie laughter poisoned her ears. "Look around, little girl. You're not out of the woods. Not yet."

Mom was right. Emily was still breathing, but her survival was not a sure thing.

With her right hand, she batted the airbag. The chemical dust that had exploded from the bag rose up in a cloud and choked her. She coughed, and her lungs ached. When she peered through what was left of the windshield, which was a spiderweb of shattered safety glass, she saw boulders and the trunks of pine trees. Literally, she wasn't out of the woods.

With the car lying on the driver's side, her perspective was off. She couldn't tell if her Hyundai had careened all the way to the bottom of the cliff or was hanging against a tree halfway down. The headlights flickered and went dark. She saw steam rising from around the edges of the crumpled hood.

In the movies, standard procedure dictated that when a car flew off the road, it would crash and burn. The idea of dying in a fire terrified her. Her gut clenched. *I have to get out of this damn car.* Or she could call for help. Desperately, she felt around for her purse. Her phone was inside. She remembered tossing her shoulder bag onto the seat beside her.

She twisted her neck, setting off another wave of pain, and looked up. The passenger side had been badly battered. The door had been torn from its hinges. Her purse must have fallen out somewhere between the road and here. Through the opening where the door should have been, she saw hazy stars and a September crescent moon that reminded her of the van Gogh painting.

Trying to grasp the edge of the roof on the door hole, she stretched her right hand as far as possible. Not far enough. She couldn't reach. When she turned her shoulders, her left arm flopped clumsily inside the black blazer she'd worn to look professional at the will reading. The muscles and joints from shoulder to wrist screamed. Blood was smeared across her white shirt; she didn't know if the gore came from her arm or the head wound matting her blond hair.

A masculine voice called out, "Hey, down there."

She froze. The monster who had forced her off the road was coming to finish the job. Fear spread through her, eclipsing her pain. She said nothing.

"Emily, is that you?"

He knew her name. Nobody she'd met with in Aspen counted as a friend. She didn't trust any of them. Somehow, she had to get out of the car. She had to hide.

Carefully avoiding pain, she used her right hand to manipulate the left. The problem was in her forearm. It felt broken. If she'd known first aid, she might have fashioned a splint from a tree branch. Her mind skipped down an irrelevant path, wishing she'd been a Girl Scout. If she'd been a better person, she wouldn't be in this mess. *No, this isn't my fault.*

She cursed herself for wasting precious moments by being distracted. Right now, she had to get away from this ticking time bomb of a car and flee from the man who wanted her dead. Holding her arm against her chest, she wiggled her hips, struggling to get free. When she unfastened the latch on the seat belt, the lower half of her body shifted position. The car jolted.

With her right knee bent, she planted her bare foot on the edge of her bucket seat and pushed herself upward toward the space where the passenger door had been. The left leg dragged. Her thigh muscles and knee seemed to work, but her ankle hurt too much to put weight on it. Inch by inch, she maneuvered herself. Using her right arm, she pulled her head and shoulders up and out. The cold wind slapped her awake. She was halfway out, halfway to safety.

Her car hadn't crashed all the way down the cliff. Three-quarters of the way down, an arm of the forest reached out and caught her little car. Two giant pine trees halted the descent. The hood crumpled against the tree trunks. The back end of the car balanced precariously.

"Emily? Are you down here?"

The voice sounded closer. She had to hurry, to find a place to hide.

She hauled herself through the opening and tumbled over the edge onto the ground. Her left leg crumpled beneath her. Behind her was the greasy undercarriage. The pungent stink of gasoline reminded her that she wasn't out of danger.

Unable to support herself on her knees, she crawled on her belly through the dirt and underbrush toward the security of the forest where she could disappear into the trees. Breathing hard, she reached a cluster of heavy boulders—a good place to pause and get her bearings. With her right arm, the only body part that seemed relatively unharmed, she pulled herself into a sitting posture, looking down at her car.

Exhaustion and pain nearly overwhelmed her. She fought to stay conscious, clinging to the rocks as though these chunks of granite formed a life raft on the high seas. She heard a small noise. Not the fiery explosion she'd been expecting, it was only the snap of a dry twig. The sound filled her with dread.

He was close.

She had to run. No matter how much it hurt, she had to get to her feet. She struggled to stand but her injured leg was unable to support her. She sat down hard on the rock. A fresh stab of pain cut through her. Before she could stop herself, she whimpered.

A silhouette of the man separated from the surrounding trees. He turned toward her. *Please don't see me. Please, please.*

"Emily, is that you?"

Quickly, he came toward her. She hoped he'd kill her fast. She couldn't take any more pain.

He sat on the rock beside her. Starlight shone on his handsome face. She knew him. "Connor."

Gently and carefully, he maneuvered his arm around her. She should have put up a fight, but she didn't have the strength, and she couldn't believe Connor wanted to hurt her.

"I already called 9-1-1," he said. "The paramedics will be here soon. I don't want to move you until they arrive with their gear to stabilize your back and neck."

He wasn't here to kill her but to save her.

She leaned against him, rested her head on his shoulder and inhaled the scent of his leather jacket. Though he felt real, she couldn't believe he was here. They'd talked yesterday. She'd been in Denver. He'd been in Manhattan. They'd both been summoned to the reading of her late ex-husband's will in Aspen, and she'd told her lawyer, Connor, not to bother making the trip. She didn't plan to attend. Why should she? She hadn't expected to receive a dime, and showing up for the reading had seemed like a lot of bother for almost zero reward.

At the last moment, she'd changed her mind. This might be her final opportunity to face the Riggs family, and she had a few choice words for them. Emily had no reason to be ashamed. Early this morning before she left Denver, she'd texted Connor about her decision to go.

"Emily, are you okay?"

"No," she mumbled.

"Dumb question, sorry," he said. "I came as soon as I could. After I got your text, I caught a direct flight from JFK to Denver, then a shuttle flight to Aspen airport, where I grabbed a rental car."

Though his deep voice soothed her, she couldn't relax until she'd told him what had happened. But her throat was closed. Her eyelids drooped.

"If I'd flown in last night," he said, "we would have made the drive together. You wouldn't have had this accident."

Accident? She wanted to yell at him that this wasn't an accident.

She heard the screech of the ambulance siren. Her mind went blank.

IN A PRIVATE hospital room in Aspen, Connor Gallagher stood like a sentry next to the railing on the right side of Emily's bed. She lay in an induced coma after four hours in surgery. Her condition was listed as critical. The doctors and staff were cautiously optimistic, but no one would give him a 100 percent guarantee that she'd fully recover. He hated that she'd been hurt. Emily had suffered enough.

Her breathing had steadied. He watched as her chest rose and fell in a rhythmic pattern. Her slender body made a small ripple under the lightweight blue hospital blanket. Though the breathing tube for the ventilator had been removed, it was obvious that something terrible had happened to her. There were three separate IV bags. Her broken left arm was in a cast from above the elbow to the fingers. A bad sprain on her left leg required a removable Aircast plastic boot. Bandages swathed her head. Her face was relaxed but not peaceful. A black-and-blue shiner and a stitched-up wound on her forehead made her look like a prizefighter who'd lost the big bout.

Being as gentle as he could, Connor held her right hand below the site where the IV was inserted. Her knuckles and palm were scraped. The doctors had said that her lacerations and bruises weren't as bad as they looked, but a series of MRIs showed swelling in her brain. The head injury worried him more than anything else.

Bones would mend. Scars would heal. But neurological damage could be a permanent disability. She'd fallen unconscious after he found her on the ground close to the wreckage of her car. During the rescue and the ambulance ride, she'd wakened only once.

Her eyelids had fluttered open, and she gazed steadily with her big blue eyes. "I'm in danger, Connor."

Her words had been clear, but he wasn't sure what she meant. "You're going to be all right."

"Stay with me," she'd said. "You're the only one I can trust."

He'd promised that he wouldn't leave her alone, and he damn well meant to honor that vow. She needed him.

Even if his presence irritated the medical staff, he would goddamn well stay by her side.

The emergency doctor who'd supervised her treatment made it clear that he didn't need Connor or anybody else looking over his shoulder. The doc had curly blond hair and the bulging muscles of a Norse god. Appropriately, his name was Thorson, aka Thor's son.

Thorson opened the door to her room, entered and went to the opposite side of Emily's bed, where he fiddled with the IV bags and checked the monitors. Connor sensed the real reason the doctor had stopped by was to assert his authority.

Without looking at Connor, Thorson said, "She's doing well."

Compared to what? Death? Connor stifled his dislike and asked, "When can she be moved?"

"Maybe tomorrow. Maybe the next day."

"Be more specific, Doctor. No offense but I want to get her to an expert neurologist."

"I assure you that our staff is highly regarded in all aspects of patient care."

Connor took his phone from his pocket. While Emily was in surgery, he'd done research. He clicked to an illustration of state-of-the-art neurological equipment. "Do you have access to one of these?"

"We don't need one."

"I disagree."

Thorson glared; his steel blue eyes shot thunderbolts. When he folded his arms across his broad chest, his maroon scrubs stretched tightly over his huge biceps.

Connor wasn't intimidated. At six feet three inches,

he was taller than the pseudogod, and he seldom lost a fight, verbal or physical. Connor returned the glare; his dark eyes were hard as obsidian.

"Tell me again," Thorson said. "What is your relationship to the patient?"

"I'm her fiancé."

"There's no diamond on her finger."

"I haven't given her a ring."

Connor avoided lying whenever possible, but he'd discovered it was easier to facilitate Emily's treatment if he claimed to be her fiancé instead of her lawyer. He'd already played the sympathy card to get her into a private room in this classy Aspen facility, where she wasn't the wealthiest or most influential patient. The nurses had been touched by the tragic story of the pretty young woman and her doting fiancé.

"No ring?" Thorson's blond eyebrows lifted. "Why not?"

"I'd like to explain in a way you could understand. But there are complex issues involved in our relationship."

That was true. Emily used to be married to his best friend, and they both used Connor as their personal attorney. Her ex-husband, a hotshot Wall Street broker, had moved his business to a more important law firm. Six weeks ago, her ex died. Complicated? Oh, yeah.

Thorson pursed his lips. "I couldn't help noticing her last name, *Benton-Riggs*. Any relation to Jamison Riggs?"

Aha! Now Connor knew why the doc was hostile. The Riggs family was a big deal in Aspen, and she'd been married to the heir, the golden boy, for seven years. She and Jamison had been separated for over a year, but the divorce wasn't final until three months ago. "Back off, Thorson."

"I should inform her family."

Hearing the Riggs clan referred to as Emily's family stretched Connor's self-control to the limit. Those people never gave a rat's ass about her. Years ago, when Jamison brought her to Aspen for the first time, Connor had tagged along. Why not? Jamison was his good buddy, a fellow Harvard grad. The two of them could have been brothers. Taller than average, they were both lean and mean, with brown hair and brown eyes. They also had the same taste in women. When Jamison introduced him to Emily, emphasizing that she was his betrothed, Connor felt his heart being ripped from his chest. She should have been with him.

The Aspen branch of the Riggs family accepted Connor, assuming that because he'd gone to an Ivy League school he came from good stock. They were dead wrong, but he didn't bother to correct them, didn't want to talk to them at all when he saw how snotty they were to Emily. She didn't wear designer clothes, didn't ski and didn't know one end of a Thoroughbred horse from another. Her laugh was too loud, and her accent was a humble Midwestern twang. Connor thought one of the reasons Jamison had married her was to drive his family crazy.

Connor growled at Thorson. "Don't call the Riggs family."

"I'm sure they'll want to be informed."

"You've seen the advance directives for Ms. Benton-Riggs, correct?" In the first years of their marriage, Jamison and Emily had asked Connor to file their living wills, powers of attorney and proxy-care forms. They had named him as the decision maker, and those papers were in effect until the divorce and the dissolution of his friendship with Jamison, who had made other arrangements. Emily, however, had never bothered to make a change. "I'm in charge of her medical care, and I don't want anyone named Riggs anywhere near her."

"You aren't thinking straight."

"The hell I'm not," Connor replied without raising his voice.

There was a light tap on the door before it opened. Standing outside was a clean-cut young man in a Pitkin County sheriff's uniform. He touched the brim of his cap. "Mr. Gallagher, I'm Deputy Rafe Sandoval. I have a few questions."

"I didn't actually witness the accident, but I'm happy to help." He gave Thorson a cold smile. "The doctor was just leaving."

As soon as Thorson stormed out, the deputy entered. Rather than hovering at Emily's bedside like the doctor, the cop motioned for Connor to join him near the door. He spoke in a hushed tone. "I don't want to disturb her while she's asleep."

"She's in an induced coma."

"But can she hear us?"

Connor had wondered the same thing. While she was unconscious, did Emily have the ability to hear his words or comprehend what he was saying? Did she know he was at her side and would destroy anyone who attempted to hurt her? "I'd like to think that she can hear, but I don't know."

Still keeping the volume low, Sandoval asked, "Why were you on that road?"

"I was on my way to the home of Patricia Riggs for the reading of her cousin's will. Unfortunately, I got a late start from New York." As soon as he spoke, he realized that the deputy would need to talk to the Riggs family about the accident. As much as Connor wanted to keep them away from Emily, the police would have to contact them. "Have you spoken to the Riggs family?"

"Not yet," he said. "Why did you pull over, Mr. Gallagher? You didn't see the accident happen, but you quickly arrived at the scene."

"There are no lights along that stretch." The two-lane road that led to Patricia's château hugged the mountain on one side. The outer lane had a wide shoulder and a guardrail at the edge of a sheer cliff. "Her headlights were shining like a beacon."

"So you stopped," the deputy prompted.

"I saw the damaged guardrail. That's when I looked over the ledge."

He'd never forget the flood of panic that had washed over him when he saw the wreckage. At the time, he hadn't known that the twisted remains of the bronze Hyundai belonged to Emily. When the headlights went off and darkness consumed the scene, he'd known what he had to do. No matter who was trapped inside, Connor had had to respond.

"This is very important, Mr. Gallagher. Did you see any other vehicles?"

"No."

"You're certain."

Connor was beginning to have a bad feeling about this visit from the deputy. It was after two o'clock in the morning. What was so important that it couldn't wait? "Is there something you need to tell me about the accident?"

The young man straightened his shoulders. His nervous manner was gone. His gaze was direct. "After my preliminary investigation, I strongly suspect that Ms. Benton-Riggs was forced off the road."

"What are you saying?"

"Someone tried to kill her."

Chapter Two

Emily knew she was asleep and dreaming hard. There was no other explanation for the weird images that popped into her mind and distracted her. She needed to wake up. There was something she had to find. The object or person or place was unclear, but her quest was urgent—a matter of life and death.

But she couldn't ignore the field of psychedelic flowers that reminded her of a Peter Max poster from the sixties, and she couldn't pause as she waltzed into a paint-splattered Jackson Pollock room with a series of framed paintings on the walls. Some were classics: melting Dali timepieces, a servant girl with a pearl earring, Tahitian women bathing by a stream. Others were by the not-yet-famous artists that she was showing in her Denver gallery. The corridor took on a more formal aspect, and it felt like she was on a personal tour of the Louvre Museum, accompanied by a grinning Mona Lisa.

Swiveling, she found herself surrounded by mist. Pink clouds spun like cotton candy around her feet and knees. When she tried to push them away, her left arm wouldn't move. From shoulder to wrist, the arm was frozen. Pursing her lips, she blew, and the haze cleared.

Connor Gallagher strode toward her. This was the Manhattan version of Connor, dressed in a tailored charcoal suit with a striped silk necktie. Though neatly groomed, his brown hair was unruly, curling over his collar. His cocoa-brown eyes penetrated her defenses.

She sighed as she placed this moment in time—a memory from several months ago when she had been trying to decide whether or not to file for divorce. She'd already left Manhattan, separated from Jamison and was working hard to establish a new life in Denver, her hometown. Connor had come all the way from New York to talk business with her. As soon as she saw him strolling up the sidewalk to her bungalow, she forgot about the contracts, documents and the prenuptial agreement she'd signed.

Connor filled her mind. She liked him…a lot. He frequently starred in her erotic fantasies. In real life, she hadn't seen him without his swimming trunks, but she suspected he could give Michelangelo's naked sculpture *David* a run for his money. In addition to her appreciation for his body, she was fascinated by his moods, the sound of his laughter and the shape of his mouth.

Her memory continued. They'd met. They'd hugged. He'd smelled warm and spicy like cinnamon. And then Connor had mentioned Jamison, asking if he also favored divorce.

She didn't give a damn what Jamison Riggs wanted. Any love she'd had for him was over. She'd been living apart from him since the night when she'd found him in

bed with the head partner from his Wall Street investment firm, a tall redhead with incredibly straight hair
and who never smiled. Jamison had expected Emily
to forgive him. He'd told her not to worry, that he was
only trying to sleep his way to the top. As if that was
supposed to be okay.

Emily huffed. She didn't believe a single word that
spilled from his lying lips. Other people had warned
her about his cheating, and it didn't take long for Emily
to find evidence of other infidelities with at least three
other women. Jamison had been having a wild, sexy
ride. Frankly, when she asked Connor to come to Denver, she'd been hoping for a taste of the same.

Sure, there were plenty of legitimate business interests they could discuss, but those weren't foremost in
her mind. She wanted Connor to embrace her, caress
her and sweep her off her feet. She deserved an affair of her own. But no! Technically, she was still married, and Connor had too much integrity to betray his
friend, even if Jamison was a dirty dog who didn't deserve the loyalty.

The day after Connor returned to his Manhattan law
practice, she'd contacted a lawyer in Denver and started
the paperwork. The divorce had taken months. So many
other things had happened, a whirlwind of events.

Her unconscious mind played calliope music. *Boop-
boop-beedle-deedle-doop-doop.* She was on a carousel,
riding a painted pony. She hadn't known Jamison was
sick until he was terminal, and she only saw him once
before he died. In light of his unexpected death, her divorce seemed cold and unfeeling. Even in a dream state,

she felt a little bit guilty. If she'd known he was ill, she might have forgiven him and nursed him through his final days. Or not.

Leaving the merry-go-round, she hiked up a grassy knoll to an old-fashioned boot hill cemetery. She'd wanted to attend Jamison's funeral and memorial service, but his maiden aunt Glenda, matriarch of the family, had made it clear that she was unwelcome. The family had kept her away, almost as though they were hiding something.

Jamison shouldn't be her problem anymore. They were divorced, and he had died. But there seemed to be a connection. Her car had been run off the road after leaving the Riggses' house. Someone wanted her dead, had tried to kill her. She had to fight back. She needed to wake up. *Oh, God, I'm too tired.*

Someone held her hand and comforted her. For now, that would have to be enough. She drifted back into silent stillness.

THE NEXT MORNING, Connor sat beside the hospital bed and patted Emily's right hand. She hadn't moved, but one of the monitors started beeping. A sweet-faced nurse whose name tag said *Darlene* came into the room and made adjustments to silence the alarm.

"Has she spoken?" Darlene asked.

"Not yet," he said. "But her eyelids have been moving. It's like she's watching a movie inside her head."

"Rapid eye movement, we call it REM. Nothing to worry about," she said in the perky tone of a confirmed optimist. "I'll notify the doctor. We don't want her to wake up too soon."

"Why is that?"

"They use the induced coma to protect the brain and let it relax while the swelling goes down. She needs plenty of rest."

Though he didn't know much about neurological sciences, he'd talked to a brain surgeon in New York who advised him about Denver-based referrals. His brain surgeon friend had given him an idea of all the stuff that could go wrong, ranging from stroke to seizure. Amnesia was a possibility, as was epilepsy. Head wounds were unpredictable and could be devastating.

He wished he could be as cheerful as Darlene, but Connor was a realist. "It seems like she wants to wake up," he said. "That's a good sign, right?"

"Well, I certainly think so." Nurse Darlene pressed her fingers across her mouth as if she'd said too much. "I'm not qualified to give opinions. But if you're asking me, this young lady is going to make a full recovery and come back to you."

And maybe she'll bring the Easter Bunny and Santa Claus with her. Connor forced a smile. The nurse wanted him to be happy, but she really didn't know—nobody knew, not for certain—if Emily would be all right. "Thank you, Darlene."

She patted his shoulder on her way out of the room. "Try to get some sleep, Connor. If you need anything, push the button and I'll be here in a flash."

Sleep was an excellent idea, but he didn't dare relax his vigilance; Deputy Sandoval had told him that Emily's accident wasn't an accident. Somebody had tried to kill her, and Connor needed to keep watch.

There was a lot to be done today. First order of business this morning would be to hire a private detective. He'd checked with the investigator who worked for his law firm in Manhattan and had got the name of a local guy. Though Connor didn't doubt Sandoval's competence, the young deputy might appreciate outside assistance from a PI—a guy who could do computer research and help him figure out why Emily had been targeted.

And Connor also needed to hire a bodyguard. The county sheriff and Aspen police didn't have the manpower to provide a cop who could stand outside her hospital room and keep watch 24/7. Also, Connor wasn't sure he trusted the locals. There was a high probability that the cops knew the Riggs family and wouldn't consider them to be a threat, even if they strolled into her hospital room carrying two crossbows and a loaded gun.

He squeezed Emily's hand and smoothed the dark blond curls that weren't covered by bandages. Even with a shiner and stitches across her forehead, she was uniquely beautiful. Her nose tilted up at the tip. Her bow-shaped lips were full. He brushed his thumb across her mouth. He'd never kissed those lips, except in a friendly way, and he was tempted to remedy that situation. Not appropriate. Kissing her while she was in a coma ranked high on the creepiness scale.

Besides, he wanted her to be awake when he finally expressed his pent-up longing. He whispered, "Emily, can you hear me?"

She said nothing, didn't open her eyes and didn't squeeze his hand.

He continued in a quiet voice, "There was a deputy who came in here last night. His name is Sandoval. He looks young but said he was thirty-two, and he's smart."

Her silence disturbed him. It was too passive. Being with Emily meant activity, laughter and a running commentary of trivial facts, usually about art.

"Sandoval investigated," he said. "He found skid marks on the road that might indicate two vehicles. One was your Hyundai, and the other had a wider wheelbase, like a truck. He couldn't re-create the scene perfectly, but he thought the truck bumped your car toward the edge. You slammed on the brake, but it wasn't enough. You crashed through the guardrail."

She must have been scared out of her mind. If Sandoval's theory was correct, a lot more investigation would be required. The sheriff's department would need to haul the wreckage of her Hyundai up the hill so the forensic people could go over it. And Sandoval could start looking for the truck that had forced her off the road.

"Do you remember? Why would someone come after you?"

His only answer came from the *blips* and *beeps* from the machines monitoring her life signs while she was in the coma.

He asked, "Did you see who was driving?"

Even if it was possible for her to comprehend what he was saying, she might not be able to identify her attacker. He continued, "I don't have evidence, but the attack on you has something to do with the Riggs family. If not, the timing is too coincidental."

He could easily imagine a member of the family or one of their minions chasing her in a truck and forcing her car off the road. It would help if he knew why. There had to be a reason.

"On the phone, you told me not to come," he said. "You expected things to get ugly between you and the Riggs family, and you didn't want to force me to take sides. Don't you know, Emily? I'm on your side, always."

Jamison's dumb-ass infidelities had pretty much ended their decade-long friendship. Connor was outraged by the betrayal of Emily. He hated the humiliation she'd endured. When she left Jamison, he'd worked with her Denver lawyer to make sure that she was financially cared for. By juggling the assets she shared with her wealthy husband, he'd finagled a way for her to have enough cash to cover her move back to her hometown of Denver, rent a bungalow and set up her own little art gallery. When that money had run dry, Connor dipped into his own pocket.

He wanted her to have a good life, a beautiful life. As a friend, he'd always be close to her. It wasn't hard to imagine being more than a friend. If only Jamison hadn't met her first in Manhattan, he and Emily would have been a couple.

After he brushed a light kiss across her knuckles, he placed her hand on the blanket, went to the window and raised the shade. The mountain view was incredible as night faded into pale dawn. If the window had been open, he would have heard birds chirping while the sunlight spread across rock faces, dark green conifers and a bright golden stand of aspens.

For a long moment, he stood and drank in the spectacular landscape. Between his Brooklyn apartment and his Manhattan office, he hadn't come into contact with this much nature in weeks. This scenery knocked him out.

He checked his wristwatch. Five minutes past six o'clock meant it was after eight in New York. He pulled out his phone to check in with his assistant. Cases were pending, but there was nothing that required his immediate attention.

It was more important to deal with Emily's medical issues. Last night, he'd culled the list of reputable neurologists and neurosurgeons down to a few. He needed to talk to them, to select a doctor for her. Then, he'd arrange for transportation to the hospital in Denver.

When Sandoval opened the door, Connor pivoted away from the window. Instantly alert to the possibility of danger, he added a mental note to his list: buy a weapon. A handsome black man with a shaved head followed the deputy into the room. He extended his hand and introduced himself. "I'm Special Agent in Charge Jaiden Wellborn, FBI."

"This isn't the first time I've seen you," Connor said as he shook SAC Wellborn's hand. "You were at a memorial service for Jamison Riggs. Two weeks ago in Manhattan."

"The service was well attended, two hundred and forty-seven people. Was there a reason you noticed me?"

"I liked your suit." Connor didn't usually pay any attention to men's clothing, but Wellborn had stood out. His attire had been appropriate for a memorial service but not lacking in style. The man knew how to dress. Even now, at a few minutes after six in the morning in a hospital in Aspen, the agent looked classy in crocodile boots, jeans, a leather jacket and a neck scarf. "Your suit was dark blue, perfectly tailored."

"Anything else?"

"You weren't milling around in the crowd and seemed more interested in taking photos with your phone. That made me think you might be a reporter. Then I spotted your ankle holster. I had you pegged as a cop, Agent Wellborn."

He didn't bother denying Connor's conclusion. "Did it surprise you to see a cop at your friend's memorial?"

"I knew there was an investigation underway." Whenever a healthy, young man succumbs to a mysterious illness, suspicions are raised, especially when the victim is filthy rich and deeply involved with complex investments and offshore banking. Supposedly, the cause of death was a rare form of cancer, but Connor didn't believe it. "The medical examiner ran a lot of tests, and the police were reluctant to release his body for cremation."

"Our only significant evidence came from the autopsy," Wellborn said. "You might have heard that the real COD was a sophisticated, untraceable poison that was administered over an extended period of time."

"Is that true?" Connor asked.

"I can't say."

"Is it classified?"

"I don't have a definite answer about the poison. He didn't suffer much until the last week to ten days, and the doctors focused on treating symptoms and saving his life rather than identifying obscure poisons."

Connor glanced toward the bed where Emily lay quietly. It didn't seem right to talk about this in front of her. Though she and Jamison were divorced, they'd been married for almost seven years. "Can we take this conversation into the hallway?"

"Go ahead," Sandoval said. "I'll stay with Emily."

After being cooped up in the hospital room with all the beeping and blipping monitors, he was glad to step outside for a moment. The pale yellow corridors and shiny-clean nurses' station were a welcome relief. He led the way around a corner and down a flight of stairs to a lounge with vending machines. Though the coffee was fresh brewed and free, the vending-machine snacks were a typical array of semistale cookies and candy. The selection looked good to Connor, which meant he must have really been starving.

He fed dollars into the machine and pulled out two chocolate bars with almonds. As he tore off the wrapping, he said, "I heard the investigation centered on Jamison's Wall Street investment firm."

"And involved several agencies, including the SEC and NASDAQ," Wellborn said as he poured himself a coffee and added creamer. "I'm with the FBI's White-Collar Crime Unit. We found a couple of shady glitches in his dealings, but nothing that rose to the level of fraud or insider trading. A few people in his office hated his arrogance. There were clients who felt cheated."

"There always are."

"Bottom line, our investigation covered all the bases. We didn't find a significant motive for murder."

"Nobody contacted me," Connor said as he peeled the wrapper off the second candy bar. "Technically, I haven't been Jamison's attorney for years, but I stay in touch with Emily. Did you investigate her?"

"Not as much as we should have. The attack last night was proof of that."

"Are you implying that Emily had something to do with her ex-husband's death?" It seemed preposterous since Emily and Jamison hadn't seen each other in months, much less had enough time together for a long-term poisoning.

Wellborn shrugged and sipped his coffee. Apparently, the feds hadn't ruled out Emily—in the role of hostile ex-wife—as a suspect.

"Why are you here?" Connor asked.

"I'm looking into the attack on Emily as it might relate to her ex-husband's death."

"As far as I know, there was very little contact between them."

"You didn't know the terms of the will. She inherited a seven-bedroom mansion in Aspen plus all the furnishings. The artwork alone is valued at nearly fourteen million."

A pretty decent motive for murder.

Connor's phone rang. The caller was Sandoval.

The young deputy's voice was nervous. "Connor, you need to get back to Emily's room. Right away."

Candy bar in hand, Connor dashed through the hospital corridors and up the stairs. Darlene the nurse beamed at him as he ran past her.

The door to Emily's room stood open.

Her bed was empty.

Chapter Three

She was gone.

The hospital machines that monitored her condition were dead silent. Connor stared at her vacant bed. Rumpled sheets were the only sign that Emily had been there. Panic grabbed him by the throat. He couldn't breathe, couldn't move. The thud of his heartbeat echoed in his ears. His fingers, white-knuckle, gripped the edge of the door.

He'd promised to never leave her. She needed his protection, had asked for his help and he had failed her. She was gone, lost.

"Son of a bitch," Wellborn muttered.

"Hush, now." Relentlessly cheerful, Darlene bounced up beside the two men and said, "This is a good thing—a blessing. Emily's family has come for her."

"The Riggs family," Connor said darkly.

"Such lovely people! Did you know our Dr. Thorson is dating Patricia Riggs? He signed Emily out."

"Where did they take her?" Connor was aware of at least three different residences, not including the one she had inherited from Jamison. "Which house?"

"I can look up the address for you." She bustled down the hall toward the main desk, talking as she went. "They hired a private nurse to take care of her at home. So thoughtful! I know Emily's in a coma, but I think she's aware of all these people who are concerned."

"The deputy that was watching her, where is he?"

"It was the craziest thing," Darlene said. "Deputy Sandoval tried to stop them."

"Why didn't he?"

"He called his boss, and the sheriff had already talked to Patricia. She told him it was okay, and the sheriff ordered Sandoval to stand down."

Connor had only been out of the room for a few moments. "How did they get this done so fast?"

"When Patricia speaks, we shake a leg."

"Ambulance," Connor said. "Are they taking Emily in an ambulance?"

"Well, of course."

He'd been with Emily when the paramedics had brought her in; he knew where the ambulances parked and loaded. If the Riggs family got her moved and settled in their home, it would be harder to pry her from their clutches. He had to act now.

He turned to Wellborn. "I've got to stop them."

"How are you going to do that?"

"Come with me and see."

"You bet I'm coming. I wouldn't miss this circus for the world."

Racing against an invisible clock, Connor flew down the corridor. Ignoring the slow-moving elevators, he dived into the stairwell, rushed down four floors and exited on the first. Wellborn followed close behind. Having him along would be useful. An ambulance driver might ignore Connor but wouldn't refuse a direct order from a fed.

At six thirty in the morning, the hallways were relatively calm. Though this was a small hospital, the floor plan was a tangled maze of clinics, waiting areas, pharmacies, shops and offices. During the four hours Emily was in surgery, Connor had explored, pacing from one end of the hospital to the other. He now knew where he was going as he dodged through an obstacle course of doctors and nurses and carts and gurneys. In the emergency area, he burst through the double doors. Outside, he spotted two ambulances.

Dr. Thorson stood at the rear of one ambulance. As soon as he saw Connor, he slammed the door and signaled the driver.

No way would Connor allow that vehicle to pull away. He vaulted across the parking lot, crashed into the driver's-side door and yanked it open.

The guy behind the steering wheel gaped. "What's going on?"

"Turn off the engine and get out."

"Those aren't my orders."

Connor had a lot of respect for paramedics and the mountain-rescue team that had climbed down the steep cliff and carried Emily to safety. Their procedures had been impressive, efficient and heroic. Not to mention that these guys were in great physical condition.

"Sorry," Connor said, "but you've got to turn off the engine."

"Listen here, buddy, I advise you to step back."

Respect be damned, Connor needed cooperation. He turned to Wellborn. "I need your gun."

"Not a chance." The fed displayed his badge and credentials. "Agent Wellborn, FBI. Please step out of the vehicle."

Further conversation became moot when Deputy Sandoval drove into the lot, his siren blaring and flashers whirling. He parked his SUV with the Pitkin County Sheriff logo in front of the ambulance. Nobody was going anywhere.

Connor stormed toward the rear of the ambulance with only one thought in mind. *Rescue Emily.* He didn't know how he'd move her from the ambulance or where he'd take her, but he sure as hell wouldn't allow her to be carried away by the Riggs family.

Dr. Thorson stepped in front of him. "Slow down, Connor."

Some people just don't know when they're beat. "Get out of my way."

"Everything has been taken care of. I've got this."

"Beg to differ."

"I assure you that—"

"Stop!" Since the doctor didn't seem to understand direct language, Connor decided to use his well-practiced techniques as an attorney whose job required him to deal with contentious personalities. He straightened his shoulders and leveled his voice to a calm monotone. "We can handle this situation in one of two ways. First, there's the legal way, where I point to the documents that state—very clearly—that I'm in charge of all decisions regarding Emily's medical care. If you don't honor the signed and notarized advance directive, rest assured that I will sue the hospital and you personally."

Thorson's tanned forehead twisted in a scowl.

"The second way," Connor said as he dropped the lawyerly persona, "is for me to kick your muscle-bound Norwegian ass."

"I'd like to see you try."

Wellborn stepped between them. "Gentlemen, let's take this conversation inside."

"I'm not leaving Emily," Connor said as he reached for the latch on the rear door. "This facility isn't secure, and there's reason to believe she's in danger."

When he yanked open the door, he saw long-limbed Patricia Riggs scrunched into the ambulance. He hated that she was near Emily, close enough to disconnect an IV line or turn off one of the machines. Thank God the paramedic was there, keeping watch.

Patricia pushed a wing of dark brown hair off her face to reveal tears welling in her eyes and streaking down her chiseled cheekbones. "Oh, my God, Connor, I can't believe this terrible accident happened to our dear, sweet Emily."

He wasn't buying the tears. Patricia was a hard-edged businesswoman, a lady shark who knew as much about the investment game as her cousin, Jamison. The only type of tragedy that would cause her to weep was when the Dow dropped four hundred points. Still, he played along, needing to get her out of the ambulance and away from Emily. He reached into the vehicle, grabbed her manicured hand and pulled her toward the open door. "You're upset, Patricia. Let's get you a nice latte."

"Are you patronizing me?"

"Let's just say that I'm as sincere as your tears."

"You don't get it." She dug in her heels. "I need to be with Emily when we take her home for the last time."

The last time? Though Emily's condition was listed as critical, none of the doctors who had seen her thought she was terminal…except for Thorson, Patricia's boyfriend.

"No more games," he growled. "Get out of the ambulance."

"But I—"

"Emily is going to recover."

"But Eric said—"

"Dr. Thorson isn't the best person to listen to. I warned him, and I'll play the same tune for you. When you interfere with Emily's care, you're breaking the law."

"Don't be a jackass." Her upper lip curled in a sneer as she came toward him. Her tears had dried, and her dark eyes were as cold as black ice. "We want the best for Emily, even if she did divorce my cousin and tear off a big chunk of the family fortune."

Connor knew precisely how much Emily had received in settlement. Considering that she'd been entitled to more in the prenup, the amount she'd actually collected shouldn't have been enough to ruffle Patricia's feathers. "You're talking about the house Jamison left her."

"It's an estate," she snapped. "Why the hell would

he leave it to her? In the past few years, they hardly ever came to Aspen. After the separation, not at all. My brother, Phillip, had to move in and take care of the property. If anyone should inherit it, it's Phillip."

"I remember when Jamison and Emily first got married," Connor said. "They stayed at the Aspen house whenever they had a spare moment. They even had a name for the place."

"Jamie's Getaway," she muttered. "Appropriate for a bank robber."

Or for a man who appreciated a place where he felt safe. Connor understood why he'd left the house to her. Jamison had been acknowledging the happier times in their marriage. His sentimental gesture wasn't enough to make up for his cheating, but it reminded Connor of why he had liked Jamison Riggs. "Here's the deal, Patricia. I make the medical decisions for Emily. If you or anyone in your family interferes, you will regret it. Jamison was once my friend, but that won't stop me from going after his family."

"You'll sue?"

"Damn straight."

Patricia stepped out of the ambulance and stalked over to her boyfriend. With her smooth dark hair and his blond curls, they made a handsome pair. Though Connor wanted to hear Wellborn question them, he turned his back and entered the rear of the ambulance. He had to see Emily, to make sure she was all right.

The paramedic was one of the men who had participated in the rescue last night. Connor was relieved to see him. "It's Adam, right? How come you're still on duty?"

"I caught a couple of z's, then came back to pick up an extra shift for a friend." He lifted a thermal coffee mug to his lips and took a sip. "Your girlfriend is looking good, considering how we found her."

He'd hooked Emily to IVs and portable machines similar to those in her hospital room, including a cannula that delivered oxygen to her nostrils. Throughout the long night, Connor had observed the digital readouts and knew what the numbers were supposed to show. He had no cause for alarm. "Are her vitals within normal range?"

"You bet. Transferring her into the ambulance went real smooth."

Still, Connor worried. "The woman who was in here, Patricia, did she get in the way?"

"You bet she did. Man, I was tripping over Riggses. There was Patricia and her bro and an older lady— maybe her mom."

"Aunt Glenda," Connor said.

"And a couple of other guys."

"Minions." The Riggs brood was a high-maintenance family, requiring many people to manage their affairs. "Did any of them touch Emily?"

"Not on my watch," Adam said. "What's got you so jumpy?"

"Just a feeling."

He was scared—an undeniable tension prickled along his nerve endings and tied a hard knot in his gut. He didn't like having emotions interfere with his actions.

Not only had he grown up tough but Connor was a lawyer who had learned how to manage his behavior. That veneer of self-control was wearing thin. In addition to feeling fear, he was angry. If he'd followed his natural instincts, he would have grabbed Wellborn's gun and blasted each and every one of the Riggses who got in his way.

No doubt, one of them was responsible for running Emily off the road. If that wasn't enough, they'd snatched her from her hospital room as soon as his back was turned. He needed to get her away from here.

He tucked a blanket up to her chin and studied her face. Her cheeks glowed with a soft pink, more color than when she'd been indoors. Her full lips parted, and she almost looked like she was smiling. He couldn't wait to see her smile for real and to hear her laughter. "It's chilly out here. How can you tell if she gets cold?"

"I can take her temperature or I can do it the old-fashioned way, like your mama did. Feel her forehead. Touch her fingers and toes."

Connor's heart had been beating fast and his adrenaline pumping hard. His own temperature was probably elevated, but he did as suggested. Her forehead was smooth and cool. The white bandages protecting her head wound and the EEG sensors contrasted her dark blond hair and her complexion. Oddly, he was reminded of her snowy-white bridal veil. On her wedding day, eight years ago, she'd been so fresh and pretty and young, only twenty-two. He and Jamison had been twenty-five, just getting started with their high-power careers. Jamison had joined his investment brokerage firm as a junior vice president and had already been able to afford to buy a small apartment in Battery Park. Connor had been in Brooklyn, jumping from one law firm to another as he built his client list and his reputation.

While Jamison was furnishing his place, he'd gone to an art gallery. That had been where he met Emily. By sheer luck, he'd found her first.

On their wedding day, Connor had forced himself to celebrate. He was the best man, after all. He had to make a toast and tell the newlyweds that they were going to be happy and their love would last forever—not necessarily a lie but not what he really wanted. He'd felt like a jerk for his interest in his best friend's bride, but he couldn't help it. He should have been the man with Emily. When it came time for him to kiss the new bride, he'd chickened out and gave her a peck on the forehead. He'd been terrified that if he kissed her on the lips, he wouldn't be able to stop.

Sitting beside her in the back of the ambulance, he took her hand, pretending to check if she was cold but hoping he'd feel her squeeze his fingers. He desperately wanted her eyes to open. There had been a few moments in her room where her lashes fluttered. REM sleep was what Darlene had called it. Emily wasn't moving now. Her face was still and serene, which he told himself was for the best. She wasn't supposed to wake up. Her brain needed time to heal.

He cleared his throat. "Is it dangerous to move her?"

"Not if I'm in charge."

Agent Wellborn poked his head into the rear of the ambulance, flashed his credentials to Adam and spoke to Connor. "I'm going to get started talking to these people before they call in their lawyers. Have you made any decisions about Emily's care?"

"I want to get her away from here. A couple of specialists in Denver have agreed to take her case. The problem is transportation." He looked toward Adam. "Can you arrange a Flight For Life helicopter?"

"I'll set it up with my dispatcher," he said. "Shouldn't be a problem, but it might take some time, an hour or more."

Connor gave a quick nod. After this incident with Thorson, he had cause to worry about the personnel assigned to take care of Emily. "I trust you, Adam. Can you come with us on the chopper?"

"Sure thing." He grinned. "I can always find something to do in Denver."

"Let's get moving," Wellborn said. "Connor, I want you to come with me when I talk to these people. You know them. You might notice something that doesn't register with me."

"I'd be delighted to do anything that might disturb the Riggs family." He glanced back at Adam. "While I'm with Special Agent Wellborn, you need to keep everyone away from Emily."

"You got it."

"One more thing," Connor said. "Patricia suggested that Emily wasn't going to wake up. Is there something I haven't been told?"

"I don't know all the details," Adam said, "but the screen on the EEG monitor shows normal brain activity for an induced coma. Seriously, dude, as long as we keep an eye on the monitors, she'll be okay. She's a fighter."

Connor agreed, "She looks like a delicate flower, but she's tough."

It seemed impossible that someone would want to murder this gentle but courageous woman. Somehow, he had to keep that fact at the front of his mind. She was in danger. It was his job to keep her safe.

EMILY COULDN'T TELL where she was, but she sensed a change in surroundings. Through her eyelids, she was aware of the light fading and then becoming bright and fading again. The calliope music still played—*boop-boop-beedle-deedle-doop-doop*. But the tone was different. And she heard a man's voice.

"She looks like a delicate flower," he'd said.

It was Connor…or had she imagined the smooth baritone? She tried with all her might to listen harder and wished she had one of those old-fashioned ear trumpets with a bell shape at the end to vacuum up sound. *Speak again, Connor. Say something else.*

There was something important she needed to tell him. At the reading of the will, there were details she wanted Connor to know.

When she'd arrived at Patricia's super-chic, nine-bedroom mountain chalet for the reading of the will, an avalanche of hostility roiled over her. Patricia hated her. Aunt Glenda had always looked down her nose at Emily. Phillip and his buddies, some of whom were good friends of Jamison, eyeballed her with varying degrees of suspicion and contempt. If Connor had been there, the atmosphere would have been different. He would have called them out and shamed them.

Though she was capable of standing up for herself, Emily didn't really want to fight with these people. Seeking refuge, she'd locked herself into the bathroom—an opulent, marble-floored facility with three sinks, gold-tiled walls, a walk-in glass shower big enough for four adults, a toilet and a bidet. She'd actually considered spending the rest of the night in there.

Staring in the mirror, she'd given herself a pep talk. *You have every right to be here. You were called to be here, for Pete's sake. You can tell these people that they're mean and interfering. After tonight, you never have to see them again.* She'd lifted her chin, knowing that she looked strong and healthy. She'd been doing renovations at the gallery and was probably in the best physical condition of her life. During the past few months in Denver, her chin-length, dark blond hair had brightened. Natural highlights mingled with darker strands. There were women who paid a fortune for this look.

She'd applied coral lipstick and given herself a smile before she opened the bathroom door. Voices and laughter had echoed from the front foyer and bounced off the ornate crystal chandelier. The sound had been disproportionately loud. She'd recoiled and covered her ears. Not ready to rejoin the others, she'd slipped down the corridor to a library with a huge desk and floor-to-ceiling shelves of leather-bound books.

The cream-colored wall opposite the curtained windows had displayed framed photos of various shapes and sizes. Many were pictures of Patricia with celebrities or heads of state or family members. None had showed Patricia's ex-husband, a man who she and Jamison had referred to as "dead to her." *Do I fall into that category?* She'd searched the wall for a sign of her relationship with Patricia. There had been several photos of Jamison, but Emily saw none—not even a group photo—with her own smiling face. Patricia had erased her from the family. So typical!

The door had opened, and a woman had stepped into the library.

Embarrassed to be caught looking at photos, Emily had taken a step back. "Are they ready to start?" she'd asked.

"Not quite yet," the woman had said. "I thought I saw you come in here. I wanted a chance to meet you before the reading."

Emily's gaze had focused on the Oriental carpet. She hadn't been really interested in mingling or meeting people. With trepidation, she'd looked up. The woman's legs were a mile long, and she was dressed in the height of Aspen chic. Her hair was long, straight and a deep auburn. Her face had had a hard expression that Emily would never forget.

"We've met," Emily had said.

"I don't think so." Not even a hint of a smile. This woman had been as cold as a frozen rainbow trout.

The first time Emily had seen her, she'd been preoccupied—tangled in the sheets and having sex with Jamison. "You're Kate Sylvester."

"Do you mind if I ask you a few questions?"

Emily hadn't refused, even though she doubted she'd be much help. She hadn't talked to Jamison in months, and she'd heard that Kate was living with him. Why had she wanted to ask so many weird questions about Jamison's finances?

In her unconscious state, she heard the distant sound of alarm bells. At Patricia's chalet, she'd been more pre-occupied with keeping her equilibrium after the Riggs family's open contempt had thrown her off her game. She hadn't given Kate a second thought.

But now? After the attempt on her life?

Everything about the will reading took on a much darker tinge.

When she woke up, she had to remember to tell Connor about this connection that spanned the country from Aspen to Jamison's New York investment firm.

Chapter Four

In a vacant office near the emergency exit, SAC Well-born assumed the position of authority behind the desk. Patricia and Aunt Glenda sat opposite him while Connor remained standing with his back against the closed door. The only thing keeping him awake was a fresh surge of adrenaline, and he thoroughly resented that the Riggs women held coffee mugs from the hospital cafeteria in their manicured hands.

He hadn't seen Aunt Glenda in four or five years. She hadn't aged, which was a testament to plastic surgery and stringent maintenance procedures. He knew for a fact that she was in her late seventies. Her straight hair—solid black without a trace of gray—was pulled up in a high ponytail, showing off her sharp features. Though the never-married matriarch of the Riggs family might be described as a handsome woman, Connor thought she looked like a crow with her black hair and beady eyes.

"Where's Phillip?" he asked.

"Dealing with another matter," Patricia said. Her upper lip curled in a sneer. She really didn't like him.

The feeling was mutual. Connor couldn't resist baiting her. "Your baby brother should be here. Whatever he's doing can't be more important than talking to the FBI."

"Phillip is accompanying Dr. Thorson." Her hostility flared. "Because of your absurd accusations, Eric is in trouble with the hospital administration. Phillip went with him, hoping to smooth the waters."

Reading between the lines, Connor figured that Phillip would get Thorson off the hook with a big fat juicy donation to the hospital. Not only was the Riggs family wealthy, but they'd been in Aspen for a long time and wielded a lot of influence. Some of the cousins were on the city council, and Phillip had considered running for mayor. Their uncaring manipulation of power made Connor want revenge. Suing them wasn't enough. He wanted blood.

Wellborn placed a small recording device on the desk. "I'll be making a permanent record of this conversation." He stated the date, the location and the people in the room.

Before he could proceed, Patricia rapped on the desktop. "Excuse me, should we have a lawyer present?"

"That will not be necessary," Aunt Glenda pronounced. "We wish to do everything possible to be helpful. I feel partially responsible for Emily's accident. When she left, I should have sent someone along with her or had her followed."

"Why is that?" Wellborn asked.

"Isn't it obvious? After hearing about her inheritance, she was so thrilled and excited that she couldn't keep her little car on the road." Glenda spoke with absolute confidence. "We'll do whatever we can to take care of Emily. That includes opening my home to her and hiring a nurse to watch over her."

Patricia backed up her aunt with a barrage of commentary, describing the facilities at Glenda's sprawling cattle ranch, which included a barn, a bunkhouse and a hangar for a small single-engine airplane—none of which seemed pertinent to the care of a woman in an induced coma. But Patricia was on a roll, babbling about how much she liked Emily and how much they had in common and many, many, many other lies.

Wellborn interrupted, "Why didn't you consult with Mr. Gallagher before moving the patient?"

Glenda held up a hand to silence her niece. "It simply never occurred to me. I don't know what Connor has been telling you, but he has no relationship with Emily."

Wellborn looked toward Connor. "I thought you were her fiancé."

"No."

Patricia took her shot. "You lied. So pathetic! You've always been insanely jealous of Jamison. You envied his success, his style and now his wife. What's the matter, Connor? Can't find a girlfriend of your own?"

Rather than going on the defensive and trying to justify his lying, he sidestepped. "Aunt Glenda is right. My relationship with Emily is irrelevant. However, her advance directive documents give me durable power of attorney and appoint me as the decision maker for her medical care. I'll be happy to show you the paperwork."

"Which brings me back to my initial question,"

Wellborn said. "Why not talk to Connor before transporting an unconscious woman to your ranch?"

Glenda looked down her beak. "How would I know he was responsible?"

"Thorson knew," Connor said. That fact was indisputable.

"But I didn't." Glenda sniffed as though she'd caught a whiff of rotten eggs. Apparently, she had no problem throwing the blond doctor under the bus, blaming the whole incident on him.

Patricia leaped to his defense. "My fiancé saved Emily's life. He's—"

"You're engaged to Dr. Thorson," Wellborn said.

"Yes, I am." Proudly, she stuck out her left hand so they could admire her flashy Tiffany-cut diamond. "We'll be married next year."

"Or sooner," Aunt Glenda said. "Patricia mustn't wait too long, doesn't want to add any more wrinkles before the wedding. She's fourteen years older than the doctor, you know."

"Please, Aunt Glenda." Patricia pinched her thin lips together. "The FBI doesn't need to know about my personal affairs."

"Agent Wellborn might want to watch out," Aunt Glenda continued. "He's a very attractive man, and he's wearing a Burberry scarf."

"You'll have to excuse my aunt," Patricia said.

"It's no secret that you prefer younger men. You're a cougar, my dear, and a successful one. You should be pleased with yourself."

"How dare you!"

"Cougar."

Their infighting made him sick. Connor hated that Emily had wasted some of the best years of her life in the company of these harpies, and he vowed to never again complain about his huge Irish family in Queens. Sure, the Gallaghers did a lot of yelling. But there were also hugs, apologies and tears. Under all their blarney and bluster, there was love.

"Ladies," Wellborn said, "I'd like to get back to the central issue. Did you move Emily on the advice of Dr. Thorson?"

"We wanted to take her to the ranch," Patricia said before her aunt could throw another barb at her fiancé. "You must have forgotten, Aunt Glenda, but we spoke to Eric about our plan, and he told us there might be a problem with the paperwork."

"I didn't forget," Glenda snapped. "My mind is as sharp as it ever was."

"Of course it is." Patricia's voice dripped with condescension, and she rolled her eyes. Not a good look for a bona fide cougar. "We were so concerned about Emily that we didn't pay enough attention to Eric's advice. It was for the best, we decided, to avoid a confrontation with Connor. Emily needs to be home and surrounded by family before she passes on."

"She's not dying," Connor said.

Patricia schooled her expression to appear sympathetic. "I understand the denial. But, Connor, you must be aware that Emily flatlined on the operating table. It happened twice. She was technically dead. Her heart stopped."

He hadn't heard this before. Though he wouldn't put it past Dr. Thorson to make up a story like this if it suited his purposes, there had been other doctors present. No one had told him that Emily was so near death. "You're lying."

"Think what you want," Aunt Glenda said. "That girl is hanging on by a thread."

It wouldn't do any good for him to explode. Connor threw up a mental wall, blocking their innuendo and deceit. Glenda and Patricia wanted Emily under their control; they'd admitted as much. But why?

"If Emily died," he said, hating the words as soon as they passed his lips, "what would happen to the house she inherited?"

"You seem to be acting as her attorney," Patricia said. "You tell us."

It was an interesting question—one he needed to research. As far as he knew, Emily had no living relations. She'd been an only child. Her parents were older when they had had Emily, and they'd died from natural causes when she was a teenager. He doubted she had a current will reflecting her divorce. There were documents he'd drawn up when she and Jamison were first married, but that was a long time ago.

A further complication when it came to ownership of the house she'd inherited was the actual transfer of property. Emily didn't have a deed. The probate court would surely step in. He handled transactions like this on a regular basis, and the paperwork was intense.

While Patricia launched into another diatribe about how her brother had been taking care of the property and deserved compensation, Wellborn leveled an assessing gaze in her direction. Connor had the sense that the good-looking black agent was accustomed to dealing with self-obsessed rich people who wouldn't stop talking. He maintained an attitude of calm. The only sign of his annoyance was the way he tapped his Cross pen as though flicking ashes from a Cuban cigar.

"Last night," Wellborn said, "was the reading of the will for Jamison Riggs. Start at the beginning and tell me everything that happened."

Patricia settled back in her chair and sipped her coffee. "I should probably start with the list of individuals who had been invited. My assistant has a copy, as does our family attorney."

Inwardly, Connor groaned. This conversation or interrogation—whatever Wellborn called it—could take hours. He couldn't spare the time. Emily needed to be moved to Denver, where he could make sure she was safe.

When Adam, the paramedic, texted him to let him know that they were ready to transfer Emily to the helicopter, he was relieved to get away from the Riggs women.

With a wave to Wellborn, he opened the door to the office. "I'll stay in touch."

IMPRESSED WITH THE efficiency of Adam and the other medical emergency personnel, Connor watched as they carried Emily on a gurney into the orange-and-yellow Flight For Life helicopter. They moved slowly and with extreme care but couldn't help jostling her.

Though she showed no sign of being disturbed, every bump made Connor think he might be making a mistake. Transporting her to Denver, where she could get the best care, seemed rational and prudent. He'd spoken to Dr. Charles Troutman, a neurologist with a stellar reputation who had taken a look at Emily's brain data and had agreed to take her case. Connor's instincts told him he was doing the right thing, getting her away from the place where she'd been threatened. But what if moving her caused her condition to worsen?

With the big cast on her left arm and the plastic boot on her left leg, she was hard to handle. But Adam and his associates managed to transfer her onto the bed where they readjusted the IVs and monitoring equipment. Connor stared at the wavy lines and the digital numbers on the screens. The emergency medical transport was equipped with all the equipment in the hospital and more. The crew included a pilot, an EMT copilot, a nurse and Adam, who vouched for the others.

Connor couldn't take his eyes off Emily. Even when she was being moved, the monitors showed very little change. Though that was what the doctors wanted— a smooth transition—he longed to see a reaction from her or to hear her speak—just a word. He wanted some kind of sign that she was all right.

When she was safely secured, belted himself into a jump seat and watched her as the chopper swooped into the clear blue skies. Through the window, he glimpsed snowcapped mountains. Soon, it would be winter. The golden leaves of autumn would be gone, and snow would blanket the tall pines and other conifers.

"You'll be better by then," he said to Emily.

"What?" Adam looked up from the equipment he'd been monitoring.

"I was talking to her," Connor said without shame. Even if she couldn't hear him, he felt the need to reach out to her and reassure her. He unbuckled his seat belt and moved closer to her. With the back of his hand, he caressed her cheek. Taking full responsibility for her, making life-and-death decisions, was the hardest thing he'd ever done.

Adam bumped his arm as he reached across her bed to slide a pillow under the plastic boot on her ankle. "Sorry, Adam, I need to step away. I've got a couple more things to check.

"We've got everything under control."

Not only did Connor appreciate the skill and competence of this young man but he trusted Adam. "You're doing a great job. If there's ever anything I can do for you, name it."

"Well, let me think." He grinned. "I'm already hooked up with a season ski pass, my rent isn't too bad and I've got a kick-ass girlfriend. All in all, my life is good."

"I'll get out of your way."

Back in his jump seat, he flipped open his laptop. He envied Adam's simple but fulfilling lifestyle. Connor had never been a laid-back guy. He had needed to fight to win a partial scholarship to Harvard, and when he was there he took on the role of a super achiever. The struggle hadn't ended with graduation. He'd worked his way through several law firms until he'd found the perfect match at Shanahan, Miller and Koch, where he was well on his way to partnership.

Lately, his fire had dimmed. During these hours he'd spent rescuing Emily, he'd felt more alive than he had in years.

Using his computer, he contacted his assistant at the law firm. Last night, he'd hired a security firm, recommended by the investigator who had done work for him in New York. The bodyguard—a former marine—was scheduled to meet them at the airport before they continued on to the hospital.

If all went smoothly, Dr. Troutman would be waiting for them at the hospital. He was associated with one of the top neurosurgeons in the country, a woman who had developed techniques to treat stroke victims. Troutman hoped Emily's condition wouldn't require an operation, but they should prepare for the possibility.

During the flight, Connor texted back and forth with his assistant—a fresh-from-law-school junior partner who was capable of handling most of Connor's caseload with minimal direction from him. Projecting that he wouldn't be back to work for at least two weeks, maybe longer, Connor suggested which cases could be postponed and which should be reassigned to other attorneys in the firm. A few years ago, when his ambitions had been burning brightly, he never would have passed on these projects. But he didn't hesitate now. He'd proven himself to be a hard worker, so that wouldn't be in question. Plus, Emily's well-being was more important.

Adam called to him, "Connor, you should come over here."

Immediately, he disconnected his laptop and went to Emily's bedside. She lay motionless, breathing steadily. The machines that monitored her vital signs hadn't changed, but the EEG monitor showed flashes of brain activity. "What's going on?"

"I'm not sure."

"Could it be the altitude?" Tension sent Connor's heartbeat into high gear. "Maybe it's the movement."

"All I know," Adam said, "is that she's waking up. The nurse wants you to put in an emergency call to the neurologist in Denver. He'll tell us what to do."

While Connor punched in the phone number, he asked, "If she wakes up, what happens?"

"Maybe nothing," Adam said. "There might be no problem at all."

"Worst-case scenario?"

"She could have a seizure. There might be an internal bleed or a clot that would cause an aneurysm."

An aneurysm and internal bleeding could lead to irreparable damage or death. As soon as Connor had the doctor on the phone, he handed it to the nurse, who rattled off a barrage of medical terminology. Sitting as close as possible, Connor held her small delicate hand and watched her face, trying to read what was going on inside her head. She looked the same as she had a few hours ago at the hospital in Aspen, except her eyelids were twitching. Her breathing became more emphatic. He saw variations in the rhythm of her heart and her blood pressure.

Keeping the desperation from his voice, he said, "If

you can hear me, Emily, I need you to listen. You need more sleep, more rest. Don't wake up, not yet."

He felt the tiniest squeeze on his hand. Had he imagined it? Though he wanted to see her awake, talking and interacting, that wasn't the best treatment for her. "Stay asleep, Emily."

Gently, he caressed the line of her chin and her stubborn jaw. She'd never been a woman who blindly followed orders or instructions. Being asleep and unable to react would never be her first choice. He tried to reassure her, telling her that there was nothing to worry about. "I've arranged for your medical care and hired a bodyguard because... You know."

Though she knew that someone had run her off the road, he probably shouldn't talk about it while she was in a coma. Her brain might pick up the threat and become alarmed, pumping out spurts of adrenaline that would cause her to wake up. He should be talking about better times, evoking positive thoughts. One topic always made her happy: art.

"There's a special exhibit at that little gallery you always liked in Brooklyn," he said. "It features posters, and they even have a couple from Toulouse-Lautrec."

While the nurse unhooked one of the IV bags, Adam said, "We've got a solution."

"What does the doctor think?"

"It's got to be the sedation. It's not keeping her in the coma. I changed the IV bag on the ambulance ride to the airport." And now the nurse changed the bag again.

"It's possible that the one I used didn't have the correct dosage to keep her asleep."

Connor doubted the wrong dosage was an accident. Patricia and Dr. Thorson had been near Emily in the ambulance. Either of them could easily have switched the bags. "Don't throw that bag away. There might be fingerprints."

"You got it." Adam stepped aside as the nurse prepared a hypodermic needle. "She's going to give Emily a shot that should keep her calm until we get to Denver. We're only about a half hour away."

The chopper shuddered. "Is it safe to do that while we're bouncing around?"

"Trust me," Adam said. "I'm usually in the back of an ambulance racing around hairpin turns at a million miles an hour. This chopper ride is smooth."

When a needle was jabbed into Emily's arm, Connor stared at the monitors. It was probably unreasonable to expect immediate results, but he needed some kind of reaction. How long would it take for the sedative to enter her bloodstream? When would he see the change? He needed to know.

Adam was back on the phone, talking to the doctor. He, too, watched the screens. The EEG showing brain activity continued to flare in multicolored bursts—green, red and yellow. Connor held his breath, waiting for a sign. After a few tense moments, her blood pressure and pulse gradually started to drop.

Adam reported the numbers to the neurologist, and

then he gave Connor a thumbs-up. "This seems to be working."

Relief breezed through him. He lifted her hand and brushed a kiss across her knuckles. "You scared me, Emily."

Her lips parted. Faint words tumbled out. "Handsome… Sleeping… Kiss."

He leaned closer. "What is it?"

Her eyelids separated. Through the narrow slits, she stared at him. And she whispered, "Snow White… Kiss."

Adam shoved his shoulder. "You heard the lady."

With a smile, the nurse concurred, "Kiss her."

Leaning over her, he planted a light kiss on her lips. This brief contact wasn't meant to be the least bit erotic, but he felt a jolt of awareness. His senses heightened. He'd been in the dark, and now a light bulb had come on.

That momentary kiss made him feel alive. He knew what had been missing in his life.

Chapter Five

He kissed me.

In every fairy tale, the sleeping beauty needed the kiss of a heroic prince to wake her, and then they lived happily forever. Emily knew better than to count on that rosy ending, but she was glad to have the magical kiss. It was a wake-up call. Now she could find the person who wanted her dead.

Hoping to bring her vision into focus, she blinked a couple of times. Connor's features became clearer. Looking at him was always pleasing—now more than ever because he was officially her hero.

His brown hair was disheveled as though he'd just got out of bed. Not that she'd know what that looked like. She and Connor had never gone to bed together. Once, on a group trip to the Caymans, they had been the first ones up and had shared a first cup of coffee before strolling across the pristine sand to wade in the shimmering blue sea. She remembered the sense of wonder and intimacy that surrounded them. Maybe she felt closer to him than any of Jamison's other friends because she and Connor didn't come from a richy-rich background. She trusted him. He was on her side, and she needed allies to help her figure out who was trying to kill her.

It was about time for her to wake up. She had a lot to tell Connor, but the poor guy looked like he hadn't slept all night. Was it only one night she'd been asleep? Was it two? She wanted to ask but got distracted as her gaze roamed over his features. Though his chin was covered with stubble and his chocolate-brown eyes were red-rimmed, he was as handsome as Prince Charming. Maybe he'd kiss her again, this time with more pressure. She remembered how he'd looked on that beach in the Caymans. He'd been wearing low-slung board shorts and nothing else. His wide shoulders and lean, muscular chest had tantalized her. Though she'd been a married woman at the time, there was no rule against looking.

And now they had no reason to stay apart. She wanted him to kiss her like he meant it. If his tongue happened to slip inside her mouth, she wouldn't mind too much.

Her lips tingled. When she tried to reach up and touch her mouth, her left arm wouldn't move. Her gaze flickered toward her left hand, and she saw a massive cast that went from her wrist all the way up past her bent elbow. It looked bad. Then she noticed an ugly gray plastic boot on her left leg. She had many injuries, but they didn't seem to hurt. Floating on a wave of euphoria, she was feeling no pain. Her eyelids drooped.

"That's good," Connor said in his soothing baritone. "Let yourself go back to sleep."

"No." She roused herself. There were things that

needed to be done, wrongs to be righted and bad guys to track down. She flexed her right arm and tightened her grip on Connor's hand. "Don't want to sleep."

"I understand," he said, "but the doctor advised that you rest."

"What doctor?" She lifted her head off the pillow to scan her surroundings and saw lots of medical equipment and windows filled with clouds and sky. This wasn't like any hospital she'd ever been in. "Where am I?"

"Helicopter," Connor said. "We're on our way to Denver, where we'll meet with a neurologist—Dr. Charles Troutman."

Her head lowered to the pillow. The edges of her vision were getting hazy. "Somebody tried to murder me."

"The police are looking into it."

"Sandoval," she said. "Deputy Sandoval."

"Wow." His fingers tightened on hers. "I didn't think you heard me talking about him. I thought you were asleep."

And she didn't remember the conversation, but the words were in her head. Deputy Sandoval had noticed skid marks on the road and the shoulder. He'd deduced that there had been two vehicles, one with a wide wheelbase.

"Forced off the road," she said, "by a truck."

"That's right."

"Did he find it?"

"Not yet, but he's looking. Do you remember anything about the truck? Did you see who was driving?"

"No."

A different speaker said, "Hey, Emily, no need to worry. Just relax. Let it go."

"Who are you?"

"I'm a paramedic," the voice said. "My name is Adam."

"I know you, Adam." His voice was familiar, and she had memories connected to him, recent memories. She parroted his words. "You said, 'Trust me.'"

Under his breath, he said, "Damn, she hears everything."

"I do." And she took satisfaction in her ability to comprehend what was happening. "Somebody gave me a shot."

"That was a nurse, and the shot was a sedative. Dr. Troutman wants you to stay asleep."

"Induced coma," she said.

They might as well be accurate in what they were saying. She wasn't taking a little catnap but had been sedated. And the doctor she'd be seeing was a neurologist, which meant she had some kind of head injury. A particularly visceral memory played in her mind. After touching a wound on her head, her fingers had been sticky with blood. More blood smeared her white shirt. Her hair had been matted.

For some reason, she'd come out of the coma. "Why…" Her awareness was fading, and she realized it was due to the sedative. She forced herself to string words together. "Why'd I come around?"

"I'm not going to lie to you," Connor said, "or hide the real circumstances. You need to know the truth so you can understand that the danger is real."

Oh, I know all about the danger. The proof was in her busted arm, her messed-up leg and God knows what other injuries. "What truth?"

"Here's what we think happened. You've been receiving a steady stream of sedatives through an IV line. When we loaded you onto the helicopter, Adam changed to a fresh bag. The medication wasn't enough. You started to wake up."

A mistaken dosage didn't seem so dangerous. As far as she was concerned, it was a minor error. She was glad to be awake, even if it was only for a few minutes. Through barely open eyelids, she studied Connor's expression. His jaw was tight and stubborn. She suspected there was something more he wasn't telling her.

The inside of her mouth tasted like the Sahara. "More. There's more to the story."

He started with a complicated description of a chase through an Aspen hospital with Thor carrying her away. *Thor? Really?* Patricia Riggs wanted to take her home to Aspen, which didn't make any sense to Emily. There was only one reason she would want to become her caretaker: to pull the plug.

Her grip on the conscious world was slipping. Vaguely, she heard Connor say something about Aunt Glenda. In *The Wizard of Oz*, Glinda was a good witch who helped Dorothy return to the people who loved her in Kansas. Not so for Glenda Riggs. She'd never helped anybody—not even her nephew Jamison after his own parents died. Her only true love was for her horses.

Emily reined in her free association and tried to understand what Connor was telling her. He said something about a sack or a bag.

"I guess I should explain," he said. "*SAC* is an acronym for *Special Agent in Charge*. His name is Jaiden Wellborn, and he works with the White-Collar Crime Unit."

As soon as he mentioned New York, her mind zoomed off on another tangent. She recalled her conversation with Kate Sylvester before the reading of the will. Jamison's former lover had wanted information from her. She'd hinted that Emily might know something about a secret account—just the sort of details an agent who worked in white-collar crime would want to know.

Kate Sylvester.

Emily felt like she'd spoken the name aloud, but Connor didn't respond. She tried again, louder this time.

KATE SYLVESTER.

Without a break, he continued his narrative, explaining how someone had switched the IV bags before takeoff. "They tried to kill you," he said, "again."

He made his point. Cutting down on the sedative dosage would cause her to come out of the induced coma, which might lead to brain damage, seizure or an aneurysm. The switch seemed like something that could be easily proved.

Who had access to the IV bags?

"We'll turn the bag over to Wellborn." Connor hadn't answered her statement, which she probably hadn't spoken aloud. Still, he'd given her a sort of answer. "The forensic people can check for fingerprints, but this evidence won't be of much value in court. It's too circumstantial. The doctor has a built-in excuse for handling equipment. And the back of the ambulance was crowded. Anyone could have touched it by accident."

But it wasn't a dead end. If changing the bag could be considered a threat, the person who was after her was one of the people in the ambulance or the hospital. Concentrating hard, she tried again to speak. *Who was in the ambulance? The hospital? Are there security tapes? Was Kate Sylvester there?*

"The good news," Connor said, "is that you don't seem to be affected by the change."

Except now I can't talk. Listen to me. You need to talk to Kate Sylvester. Mentally, she yelled the name over and over. *KATE SYLVESTER. KATE, KATE, KATE!*

Her voice was gone. What if this was a permanent condition and she was never to speak again? If she was able to hear the whistles of birdsong and music and other voices, her own silence wouldn't be much of a sacrifice. Vision was the sense she prized the most. Her greatest pleasure came from appreciation of art or by watching a sunrise. She couldn't imagine a life without ever seeing Connor again. He was well on his way to becoming an essential part of her world.

"We're here," he said, "coming in for a landing."

I can tell. When the chopper dipped, her world shifted. Being supine on an aircraft was very disorienting.

"This helipad is close to the hospital," Adam said. "I can see the ambulance at the edge of the landing circle, waiting for us."

"Will you come with us?" Connor asked. "I want to make sure her transfer goes smoothly."

"Me, too. And I'd like to meet Dr. Troutman."

That's a funny name, Troutman. Wonder if he looks like a fish.

Underwater images played in her mind. She'd always liked *The Little Mermaid.* Rational thought faded from her mind.

NOT ONLY WAS the ambulance waiting at the edge of the helipad, but other people were there to greet them. A man and a woman, both wearing aviator sunglasses, stood beside a black SUV with heavily tinted windows. The man wore a dark gray sports jacket and loosely knotted necktie. The tall blonde woman was dressed in a black pantsuit with a white blouse. Her rigid posture and intense attitude made Connor think that she'd been in the military.

They both looked tough, and Connor hoped they'd been sent by the security company he'd contacted. He could use some muscle on his side. While Adam and the other ambulance driver transferred Emily from the chopper to the ambulance, he approached the SUV.

The man in the suit made the introductions. "Connor Gallagher? We're from TST Security. I'm Robert O'Brien, and this here is T. J. Beverly. She's your bodyguard."

Connor shook hands and listened while O'Brien did a snappy run-through of his credentials, which included computer skills and twelve years as an LAPD detective.

Beverly's resume was six years as a bodyguard and nine as a marine, honorably discharged.

When Connor led them to the ambulance and introduced Adam, the paramedic bonded immediately with the tall blonde woman. They exchanged salutes. He murmured, *"Semper fi."*

"Oo-rah," Beverly said under her breath.

An interesting development. Connor hadn't suspected that the easygoing Adam was a former marine, but that background made sense. When Adam wasn't skiing, he was still in the business of rescuing people in danger.

Connor paused beside the gurney where Emily lay still and calm—a gentle presence in the midst of all the medical equipment. "This is Emily Benton-Riggs. She's in an induced coma. We're taking her to Crown Hospital, where she'll be under the care of Dr. Troutman."

"I'm going to need a whole lot more information," O'Brien said. "I heard there was a fed assigned to the case."

"As soon as she's settled in her hospital room, I'll fill you in."

"Sure thing," O'Brien said.

Connor's concern was, first and foremost, for Emily's well-being. All this shuffling around couldn't be good for her. He nodded to Adam, giving him the signal to load her into the ambulance and turned back to the team from TST Security. "I have an unusual request. Whenever possible, I want our conversations about the investigation to take place in Emily's presence. She looks like she's unconscious, but she hears more than you'd think. And she wants to keep informed about what's happening."

"Have you had a chance to question her?" O'Brien asked.

"Not really," Connor said. "She was awake for a few minutes but didn't say much. I had the feeling there was something more she wanted to tell me."

When he climbed into the rear of the ambulance, he was surprised to find Beverly right behind him. She pulled off her sunglasses. "From now on, I stay with Emily."

Though Connor appreciated Beverly's dedication to duty, the back of the ambulance was seriously crowded. "It's okay. I can take care of her."

"No offense, sir. But this is my job. I know what's best."

In usual circumstances, Connor would have ceded control to someone with more expertise, but he was tired and irritable and didn't want to be crammed into the ambulance. "It's only twenty minutes—a half hour at most—to the hospital. What could go wrong?"

"There's potential for a naturally occurring problem, such as a malfunction of the ambulance or a collision." Without breaking a smile, Beverly continued, "If someone is deliberately trying to hurt Emily, this vehicle could be targeted by a sniper. We could be carjacked. There are a number of places along the route that could be rigged with explosives. Do you want to hear more?"

Horrified and fascinated, Connor nodded. "Tell me."

"You can't trust anyone. For example, how much do you know about the ambulance driver and the paramedic?"

The ambulance service had been arranged by the hospital, but Connor got the point. "You're saying that I can't trust anyone."

"Correct," Beverly said. "For your information, we ran computer checks on these men before your arrival. They're clean."

"I'm glad you're working for me."

"In my six years as a bodyguard, I've never lost a client. Never had one injured."

Connor believed her.

On the drive to the hospital, Connor and Adam explained the switch in IV bags to Beverly, who thought that technique seemed too sophisticated when compared to running Emily's car off the road with a truck. Were two different people trying to kill her?

Connor pointed out the similarity. "If either of these attempts had succeeded, her death could have been considered accidental."

"True." She frowned. "You suspect the family. Why?"

"Just last night, Emily inherited a mansion in Aspen, complete with furnishings—millions of dollars' worth of property and artworks."

"That's a motive," Beverly agreed.

In spite of the many dire possibilities, they arrived at the hospital in one piece. While Beverly scanned the unloading area, searching for potential threats, Connor kept his eye on Emily. She looked much the same, beautiful and unconscious.

In the hope that she could hear him, he whispered, "We're almost there. You're doing great."

When he looked toward the hospital staff who took over Emily's care, he noticed a woman in scrubs with straight red hair. She caught his eye and then quickly looked away. He'd seen her before, but couldn't remember when.

Before he had the chance to approach her or to alert Beverly, the monitors attached to Emily changed in rhythm and pitch. The sound touched a nerve in Connor. Panic rushed through him. Noise became a blur. His field of vision zoomed in on Emily.

Her jaw clenched as she threw her head back. Shivering and twitching, a convulsion racked her body. Adam and the other paramedic went into action.

How the hell could this happen? Why? Why now? They'd been so close to safety. Connor had almost allowed himself to relax. He jogged beside the gurney as they charged through the doors into the ER.

Chapter Six

While the ER staff went into high gear, a sense of help-lessness paralyzed Connor. He couldn't think, couldn't move. There was nothing he could do but stand and watch as Emily's monitoring equipment fluctuated, flashed warnings and crashed. ER personnel swarmed the gurney, and Beverly inserted herself into the mix, making it her business to limit their numbers.

Connor allowed himself to be shoved out of the way, but he didn't leave. He found a position where he could remain in visual contact with her, just in case she looked for him. It pained him to see her struggle. Her lips drew back from her teeth. Her eyes bulged open. Straining, she stared at the ceiling. Her chest rose and fell in rapid gasps. Her limbs shuddered.

Desperately, he wanted her pain to stop. If he'd been a praying man, he would have dropped to his knees, begged forgiveness for past sins and promised to be a good person henceforth. He ought to be able to do something like that—to make a deal with God. Draw-ing up contracts was his special expertise. He'd gladly offer the moon and the stars. He'd give anything to make her well.

But life didn't work that way. He didn't know what had triggered her seizure, didn't know how long it would last or how to control her muscle spasms. His only certainty: it wasn't fair. She'd done nothing wrong, didn't deserve this.

Gradually, the episode passed. The tension left her face. Her jaw relaxed. The lines on her forehead smoothed. The sense of urgency faded as she was moved into the intensive care unit to recover. At Beverly's insistence, she was placed in a tight little room with curtains across the front.

A tall, lean man wearing a white lab coat escorted Connor away from her bed and introduced himself as Dr. Charles Troutman. His narrow face, deeply etched with wrinkles, seemed intensely serious, until he smiled. The doctor had an infectious grin.

"Some people call me Fish," Troutman said. "I'd rather you didn't."

"Whatever works for you," Connor replied. "How is she?"

Troutman glanced over his shoulder at the bed. He'd left the curtain open so they could see her. "Emily doesn't appear to be someone who gives up easily. She's a survivor."

Though Connor took comfort in that description, he wanted more. "Give me your medical diagnosis."

"Brain trauma. That's all I can say right now. Our first order of business is to get her stabilized."

Though Connor knew next to nothing about medical procedures, he'd consulted with an East Coast neurologist he often used as an expert witness. "You were highly recommended."

"Thanks." Troutman's smile dimmed. "According to Emily's advanced directives, you're the decision maker when it comes to her treatment. Correct?"

"That's right." Connor had a bad feeling about what might be coming next.

"I want you to be prepared. After examination, we might determine that Emily needs brain surgery, which is, of course, a life-threatening operation. I'll need your authorization for that procedure."

His gut clenched. This responsibility was too much. "Can you guarantee she'll be okay?"

"I wish I could make you an ironclad promise," he said, "but I'm a doctor, not a psychic."

Connor hedged. "You don't need an answer right now."

"No, I don't. But it's wise to consider all possibilities." Troutman gave him another gentle smile. "You look tired, Connor. I've scheduled her examination for four o'clock. You might try to get some sleep before that."

Not a bad idea. If Emily was okay, it wouldn't hurt for him to step away. He slipped behind the curtain into her ICU cubicle and moved into the spot next to the bed railing where he could hold her hand. The machines and monitors played their familiar symphony. Her breathing seemed normal. Her color was good.

He glanced over at Beverly. "I'm going to find a bed and catch a couple hours' sleep."

"Where?"

"It's a hospital. One thing they've got here is beds."

Beverly pulled out her cell phone and tapped in a number. "I'll tell O'Brien to arrange a place for you to rest."

"Don't bother." He didn't even need a bed. As soon as Connor had started thinking about sleep, the exhaustion he'd held at bay nearly overwhelmed him. "I can flop down on one of the couches in the waiting room."

"This isn't about your comfort."

"Then what's it about?"

"Don't be an ass, Connor. You're in danger."

What the hell was she talking about? "Me?"

"I'll put it bluntly. Somebody wants Emily dead, and you're in the way."

Connor hadn't thought of himself as being vulnerable, but Beverly was right. "I'll do things your way."

"Damn right you will."

"I didn't even know O'Brien was at the hospital."

"He's been busy on his computer. We need background checks on all the personnel who have contact with Emily. It's too easy to slip into a pair of scrubs and get into a hospital. If they haven't been cleared, then don't get close."

Connor appreciated the hypervigilance. Hiring this security company was probably the smartest move he'd ever made. While they were in charge, nothing bad would happen to Emily or to him. Not on their watch.

IN THE MEDICAL building adjoining the hospital, O'Brien directed him to a private office with a door that locked.

Better yet, there was a back room with a cot and a bath-room with a shower.

Connor got comfortable on the bed. He should have been asleep in a minute. Instead, his brain was wide-awake, doing mental calisthenics as he considered the central question: Why had someone tried to kill her?

Depriving her of her inheritance from Jamison made a solid motive, but it seemed too obvious, too easy. No matter what he thought of the Riggs family, they weren't idiots. They had to know they were suspects. If the truck that had run her off the road was found, the driver would be tied to the crime. For a moment, Con-nor was tempted to bolt from the cot and put in a call to Sandoval for an update on his investigation. Not now. He needed to sleep—to reboot and refresh his thinking.

Breathing deeply, he replayed what had happened from the moment she'd called him in New York until a few moments ago. So far, Connor was okay with the major decisions he'd made. Getting her away from Aspen was smart. His security team was top-notch. Troutman seemed competent.

Doubt arose when Connor considered what came next. He might have to give the green light on her brain surgery, a dangerous operation. How could he do that? So much could go wrong. He held Emily's future in his hands. If he made the wrong call, she might die or be paralyzed for life or lose her memory or any number of other negative outcomes. The blame would be laid at his doorstep. Somehow, he had to get this right.

Still not comfortable, he shifted position on the cot. In his work, he was accustomed to taking risks into account and advising people about life-changing decisions. But those people weren't Emily. What was best for her? If she was awake and alert, would she want the surgery?

There were other decisions as well, a lot of balls in the air. When the medical procedures were over and done, she was going to need help. In the worst-case scenario, she might never awaken from the coma and would require full-time nursing. A shiver stiffened the hairs on his forearms. He hated to think of Emily—a vivacious, energetic woman—being physically limited. Whatever she needed, he'd arrange for her. And he'd replace her car. And her art gallery would need overseeing.

None of those tasks were as important as nailing the person who was responsible for the three attacks. The first had been on the road. The second was on the Flight For Life chopper when her sedation had been altered. And now the seizure. It had to be connected to the other two attempts and had scared the hell out of Connor.

Her survival was his number one concern.

There were a million reasons why he wanted her to recover. Though they'd been friends for years, there had always been a chasm between them. She'd been his best friend's wife, and Connor had no right to interfere with that relationship. Now that barrier was gone. Actually, she'd been divorced for months, and he could have made his move sooner. He'd been on the verge of contacting her when Jamison died. That set him back. But not again, nothing else would stand in his way. Finally, he could act on the physical attraction that had always simmered between them.

He thought about gathering her into his arms and kissing her, gently at first and then harder while he stroked her lightly freckled shoulders and combed his fingers through her hair. He'd seen her in a bikini and loved her breasts—they weren't too big, but round and full. When he and Emily finally rolled into bed together, he didn't think she'd need coaxing. She wanted him, maybe not as much as he wanted her, but enough. He imagined her smooth, slender legs entwined with his. Her firm torso would rub against his chest. For years, he'd dreamed of these sweet, sensual moments.

His sleep on the cot was filled with fantastic dreams. It felt like only a minute had passed when O'Brien tapped his shoulder and announced, "Fish is almost ready to start the neurological exam."

"Fish?"

"Troutman," O'Brien clarified. "It's almost four."

Connor had been asleep for five hours. "Coffee?"

"Yeah, I'll grab some. Why don't you take a shower?"

Connor dragged himself from the cot to the small bathroom with the even smaller shower. This was definitely a no-frills cleanup, but the steaming hot water felt deluxe. He stuck his face under the showerhead and washed away the grime and sweat.

While sleeping, his brain had been super productive. Not only had he engaged in wild, intense fantasies about sex with Emily but he'd also remembered something Jamison had mentioned before he got sick.

The timing of his last face-to-face meeting with Jamison had been odd. A few weeks after the divorce was final, Jamison had showed up at Connor's office, saying that he was in the neighborhood and they should have a drink. They hadn't been close for some time, but he went along for old times' sake. Trying to avoid a drawn-out conversation at a bar, Connor had opted for coffee. Their conversation had turned to Emily.

"The divorce is almost final," Jamison had said. "Good news for you."

Guardedly, Connor had replied, "I'm not sure what you mean."

"You've always had the hots for my wife and—"

"Ex-wife," Connor had corrected.

Jamison had glared at him over the rim of his coffee mug. "You can make your move, buddy boy. Plead your case. With your working-class background, you have more in common with her than I ever did."

He'd almost sounded jealous, but Connor hadn't credited his former friend with that level of sensitivity. Jamison had betrayed and disrespected Emily. He hadn't deserved her. "I don't need your permission."

"Let me give you a little warning. She thinks she's done with me, but she's not. I'm still calling the shots." He'd looked around the coffee shop. "They'd all do well to remember that. I hold the purse strings. I'm in charge."

At the time, Connor had chalked up Jamison's thinly veiled threat to a shout-out from his ego, letting Connor know that he had a hold on Emily. But maybe the warning had had a wider implication. Jamison's reference to purse strings might have applied to the property in Aspen, or it might be part of the FBI investigation undertaken after Jamison's death by Agent Wellborn.

After his shower, Connor slipped into a fresh shirt that O'Brien was considerate enough to bring for him. He nodded to the security man. "Thanks for the change of clothes."

"I learned to carry extra shirts when I was LAPD." He looked up from his tablet computer. "There's nothing worse than smelling your own stink, especially when there's blood."

"Did I have bloodstains on my shirt?"

"You rescued Emily from a car wreck. I'm guessing the blood belonged to her."

It had been one hell of a day, not even twenty-four hours. When he took a good, hard look at his leather jacket, Connor saw it was in serious need of dry cleaning. "What are you searching for on the computer?"

"Filling in background on the Riggs family and poking around into Jamison's finances—the stuff that has Wellborn involved."

"The FBI couldn't dig up anything on him," Connor said.

"Which doesn't mean it's not there."

"Have you been in touch with Sandoval?"

"He's a good man, doing the best he can. Most of his day was spent by dragging her Hyundai up the cliff."

"What about the truck?" Connor asked.

"He found black paint chips stuck on the rear fender, suggesting that she was hit and forced off the road. He put out an alert to all the local law enforcement and vehicle repair places. Nobody saw the truck."

Connor followed him through the medical building and into the hospital. On the far end of the first floor, they entered a suite of offices, examination rooms and operating theaters for the neurology department. He and O'Brien looked through an observation window at a large room with dozens of machines with dials, gauges and screens.

Still unconscious, Emily sat in a chair that resembled a recliner. Her head was immobilized with a contraption that reminded him of headgear his youngest sister had worn when she had braces. Emily's good arm was strapped down. Like a kick-ass guardian angel, Beverly kept watch, hovering near the door. Troutman and three other doctors buzzed around the room, hooking and unhooking various pieces of equipment. When Troutman spotted Connor in the window, he came out to talk to him.

"The exam is going very well," he said. "She's already undergone a series of X-rays and MRIs. The swelling on her brain has gone down. We found no clots, blockages or aneurysms. Also—I can't stress how positive this is—she has no tumors."

"What about the seizure? Could she have been attacked again?"

"I can't say for sure, but we'll be doing blood tests. My best guess is that she had a reaction to other medication, perhaps the sedative. I see no indication that she'll have another event."

All this positive news made Connor suspicious. Things were going too perfectly. Gazing into the examination room, he looked for signals of impending disaster. "And what are you doing now?"

"A thorough analysis of her brain activity. Would you like a detailed explanation?"

"Give it to me in layman's terms."

"So far, everything is within normal range. She might have some short-term memory loss, might need some physical rehab, but there doesn't appear to be any serious damage."

"No need for an operation?" Connor held his breath, waiting for the answer.

"None." Troutman charmed him with a smile. "We don't need to keep her in a coma anymore. As a matter of fact, it's better if she's awake for some of our testing. We're bringing her around right now."

"You're waking her up?"

"That's right."

Connor had to restrain himself before he gave Troutman a high five. This was the best news ever. Emily was coming back to him.

O'Brien spoke up. "I've got a question, Doc. How come the people in the examination room aren't wearing masks and operating clothes?"

"These examinations are external. We're wearing scrubs because they're as comfortable as pajamas and these exams take a long time. As you can see, your friend Beverly didn't change from her street clothes."

"Is it okay if I come into the room?" Connor said.

Troutman hesitated for a moment before he nodded. "You need to be quiet and stay out of the way."

"You've got my word."

He tiptoed into the room behind Troutman and stood beside Beverly. Troutman didn't bother to introduce him as he rejoined his colleagues, which didn't matter in the least to Connor. He was focused—100 percent—on Emily. He noticed a slight movement of her right foot inside a heavy sock. The fingers of her right hand twitched.

She was waking up, coming back to him.

Not more than ten minutes later, he watched in awe as her eyelids fluttered. With a gasp, she opened her eyes, looked directly at him.

Desperately, he wanted to speak, to tell her that everything was taken care of. He wanted to cross the room in a single bound and kiss her again.

Her lips were moving. She was trying to talk.

Though he'd promised not to get in the way, Connor took a step toward her. He spoke softly. "What is it, Emily? What do you want to say?"

Her voice was little more than a whisper. "Find Kate Sylvester."

Chapter Seven

Seated in the medical version of a recliner chair, Emily struggled to be alert and coherent, and could only mumble a few odd words. *Find Kate Sylvester.* Explaining Kate's involvement would take an effort that was, for the moment, beyond Emily's capability. At least she'd alerted Connor to the problem.

Though her vision was hazy, she watched as he came closer. She blinked, trying to bring him into sharp focus. The lighting in this room—an examination room?—was intense, and she could see every detail of his face from the character lines lightly etched across his forehead to the stubble outlining his jaw. His dark eyes compelled her to gaze into their depths and find comfort. When he captured her right hand in his grasp, her heart took a little hop. She tried to turn toward him but found herself unable to move her head.

His smooth baritone cut through the other voices and the mechanical sounds of monitors and other equipment. "It's good to have you back, Emily. I missed you."

"Me, too."

"I'm guessing that you want to get up and run around."

"Good guess."

"You'll have to wait awhile longer. These medical people have questions they need to ask and more tests to run."

Testing was okay, but she wanted to tell him that she did not, under any circumstances, want to be put back into a coma, not that she was in a position to make demands. "What questions?"

"Do you remember when we talked about Dr. Troutman?"

"Fish," she said.

A tall, pleasant-looking, older man in turquoise scrubs and a white lab coat stepped into her field of vision. "If *Fish* works for you, I'll answer to that name."

"Nice Fish."

Her mouth felt like she was grinning, but she wasn't sure what her muscles were actually doing. Apart from an occasional twinge, she seemed disconnected from her physical self. The only real sensation came from Connor's gentle pressure on her fingers.

When Fish asked him to move away, she tightened her grip and protested, "No."

"Emily, I know you've had a rough time," the doctor said, "but I'm in charge. You need to do as I say."

"Please, Fish. I just need a minute with Connor."

Reluctantly, he took a step back. "Make it quick."

Connor leaned down. "Is there something you need to say?"

"About Kate." Concentrating hard, she forced herself to put together a sentence. "I saw her when I was being brought out of the ambulance. She was there."

Connor swore under his breath. "She has red hair, doesn't she?"

"Yes."

"I saw her, too. At the time, I didn't know who she was, but she was there. She's here." He straightened up. "I'll make sure she doesn't get close to you again. Right now, you need to cooperate with the doctor."

"Don't leave me, Connor."

"I'll stay nearby."

He went across the room and talked to a man with a buzz cut and square shoulders. She'd seen this man before. Somehow, she knew he was a friend.

The doctor started in with his coordination and reflex questions, having her look to the right, then to the left. Upon his instruction, she wiggled her toes and fingers. Though these seemed like basic kindergarten exercises, she was proud of her success. When she glanced toward Connor, his expression was encouraging and kind without being patronizing.

The clouds of confusion that had obscured her thinking faded and gradually disappeared. She was nearly awake. The world began to make sense to her. The downside of regaining consciousness was the realization that her body had been badly injured. When she took a deep breath, her ribs ached. Her left arm was immobilized from biceps to fingertips in a massive cast, and the lower portion of her left leg was encased in a plastic boot.

She interrupted Fish to ask, "My leg. Is it broken?"

"According to your chart, you have a sprained ankle."

"Can I walk?"

He gave her a steady, assessing look. "Why do you ask?"

"I need to get out of the hospital so I can figure out who's trying to kill me."

His grin was charming. "You're joking."

"Am I laughing?"

"In due time, Emily, you'll recover."

"It needs to be sooner than later." She didn't know how long she'd been out of commission. Whether it had been a week or only a few hours, she needed to get in gear and investigate before all the clues dried up and the trail that led to the truth went cold. "What time is it? As soon as we're done here, I could get started."

The doctor glanced toward Connor. "You want to handle this?"

Connor stepped up, and her spirits lifted. Surely, he'd understand, and he'd be able to explain to the doctor. "Tell Fish," she said. "Tell him that I need to go after the bad guys."

"Here's the deal, Emily. There's a full-scale investigation underway with a deputy in the mountains and an agent from the FBI. Also, I hired a private detective. And I want you to meet Beverly." He gestured toward the tall woman who stood at the door. "She's your full-time bodyguard. For now, we need to let them do their jobs."

While she'd been unconscious, Connor had covered the bases. Skilled people were solving the crime, and she was protected. Though she was grateful, she didn't intend to sit quietly in the corner and watch.

While she was with Jamison, he'd always told her to sit back and relax because he had taken care of everything. Following that particular direction hadn't turned out well for her, and she didn't want to be a bystander anymore. This was her life. She'd been threatened and needed to take part in the investigation, to point them in the right direction. "There are things I know that nobody else does. That's why they're coming after me."

"I believe you," he said. "And you'll be able to investigate after you recover. You survived one hell of a crash."

"My car?"

"Totaled."

"That's enough," Dr. Fish said as he nudged Connor toward the door. "Emily, I need for you to pay attention to me."

"Please don't put me back into a coma." Though tired, she didn't want to sleep anymore. "I've got to stay awake."

"So far, your progress is encouraging," he said. "After we're done here, we should be able to move you from ICU into a regular room. Maybe we can bring you some food."

An enchilada with guac on the side. The thought of melted cheese and mashed avocados made her mouth water, even though she doubted that the hospital kitchen would be able to whip up spicy food. She was definitely hungry. Anything would taste good.

Before they got back to the tests, she heard a commotion at the door. Angry voices argued with each other. She couldn't see clearly but thought there was some shoving.

Dr. Fish appeared to be an extremely patient man, but this was the last straw. He pivoted toward the door and snapped, "What the hell is going on?"

"It's me. It's Phillip."

"Phillip Riggs," she mumbled under her breath. He had a lot of nerve showing up here. Typical of the over-privileged Riggs family, he thought it was okay for him to barge into a room where she was undergoing a medical procedure. She ought to have her bodyguard throw him out on his ass, but his sudden arrival made her curious. "What are you doing here?"

"I was worried about you."

Liar! They'd never been close. More the opposite, he spent all his time skiing and sneered at her for not being interested in a sport she'd never been able to afford when she was growing up in Denver. Patricia's younger brother was more childish than any grown man had a right to be. "Give me another reason."

Fish stepped between them. "This is unacceptable. Get out."

"Wait," she said. "Let him answer. Why are you here, Phillip? Is it about the will?"

"Not now," Fish said. "When I've finished my examination, you can play detective, but this is my facility, and I'm in charge."

"Yes, sir," Beverly said. "I'll remove Phillip and hold him until he can be interrogated."

"But I drove all the way down from Aspen," Phillip said. "If I can just get a signature from Emily, I'll be on my way."

The bodyguard muscled Phillip out the door with a comment about hospital security and the cop who was stationed at the front entrance. Emily was glad to see that Connor had stayed behind to be with her. She looked up at the doctor and said, "I'm sorry."

"Let's finish up here."

Though anxious to find out what was going on with Phillip, Emily did her best to behave like a model patient, while Fish and his team went through more tests and monitoring. At one point, she was rewarded by having the headgear removed and the other restraints that held her in place unfastened. Her tension relaxed. She lifted her right arm—just because she could—and flexed her fingers. What did Phillip want her to sign?

He was nuts if he thought she would help him out. Emily didn't consider herself to be a vindictive person, but she wasn't inclined to do any favors for the Riggs family.

Vaguely aware of her surroundings, she was loaded onto a gurney and moved from the examination room to another location and then another. She closed her eyes and rested while she was transported on the medical version of a magic carpet ride. Visions of Aladdin danced at the edge of her consciousness, but she didn't allow herself to dive into a full-blown *Arabian Nights* fantasy. Emily needed to be alert.

Every time she looked up, Connor was there, hovering at her side. He didn't look like Aladdin, and there was no way she could imagine him wearing flowing pants and shoes with turned-up toes. But he was clearly her hero.

Throughout all her troubles and her divorce, Connor had provided the shoulder for her to lean against. He'd held her hand. Most of all, he'd listened. Even though Jamison had been his best friend, Connor had sided with her. Before she drifted off to sleep, she reminded herself to tell him about the secret account Kate had mentioned in Aspen.

EMILY WAS SITUATED in a private room on the fifth floor with a partial view of the mountains west of town, and she was sleeping. Connor stood by her bed and gazed down at her. Most of the monitoring equipment had been removed. Apart from the obvious casts, she looked mostly normal. Though the wound on the left side of her forehead near her hairline was stitched and the swelling had gone down, her left eye was still black-and-blue.

His preference would have been to talk to Phillip himself and send the little jerk back to Aspen, but Connor knew Emily would be furious if he deprived her of an opportunity to be part of the investigation. She was so adamant about Kate Sylvester, who had managed to blend in by wearing scrubs. What was the Wall Street broker up to?

Beverly and O'Brien had been in the hallway talking. They returned to the room together, and O'Brien spoke up. "I'm wasting my time in Denver. I should be in Aspen, following up with Sandoval and talking to the Riggs family."

Connor shuddered at the thought. "Not a fun job."

O'Brien shrugged. "Somebody's got to do it. Before I head out to the mountains, I wanted to check out Emily's house for clues."

"I'll come with you."

Troutman wanted to keep Emily in the hospital for observation and physical therapy with her sprained ankle. He'd suggested picking up some of her clothing from home—comfortable stuff, like pajamas and sweat suits. "When she wakes up, I'll find out where she keeps the spare keys," said Connor.

"Or I can pick the lock," O'Brien offered.

"That works for me. Also, I'd like to get my hands on a weapon."

Connor noticed when O'Brien and Beverly exchanged a glance. Was it that obvious that he wasn't a marksman? "Is there a problem?"

"We'd need to get you a concealed carry permit," Beverly said. "Do you know how to handle a firearm?"

"My cousin is a cop in Queens. I've fired a Glock before, but you're right," Connor said. "I'd appreciate if you could take me to a shooting range for practice."

A small voice rose from the hospital bed. "Me, too."

Connor went to her side. "What is it, Emily?"

She aimed her forefinger at him and fired an imaginary shot with her thumb. "I could use some time on a practice range."

He wasn't sure if the world was ready for Emily Benton-Riggs, armed and dangerous. But he decided it was best if he humored her. "Sure thing."

After a bit of fumbling around, they adjusted her bed so she was sitting up. Her blue eyes were bright.

Her smile was surprisingly alert as she greeted Beverly and O'Brien.

"I'm ready," she said. "Let's get Phillip Riggs in here."

Connor didn't bother arguing. He glanced at Beverly and asked, "Where did you take the little weasel?"

"I left him in a waiting area and told him I'd call if Emily wanted to see him."

"And I do," she said.

She whipped out her phone. "I'm on it."

While Beverly made the call, Emily said to Connor, "My spare house key is hidden under the plastic garden gnome on the porch. Since you're going by the house, I'd really like for you to bring me the blue bathrobe and the moisturizing lotion in the pink container."

Under his breath, O'Brien commented, "Hard to believe she heard us talking. That lady has a great set of ears."

"My vision is pretty good, too."

"You're an art dealer," Connor said. "You've got to be able to see."

"Finding a great piece of art requires more than an ability to discern brushstrokes," she said. "It's more about the emotions evoked. Art can make you cry or laugh or shrink inside yourself to find the truth. There's a woman I'm working with who's a genius. I can't wait to launch her onto the scene in New York."

Emily's commentary on the world was something Connor had always enjoyed. With very little provocation, she could go on and on—a talent she attributed to being an only child who didn't have siblings to babble with when she was young. The words had been building up since she was a baby, and she welcomed any opportunity to let down the floodgates and talk.

Her cheerful demeanor transformed as soon as Phillip stepped into the room. He gave her a sheepish grin, pushed his sun-streaked brown hair off his forehead and bobbed his head. "Hey, Emily, it's good to see you sitting up."

She wasted no time getting to the point. "Why are you here?"

"I don't know much about finances." He almost sounded proud of his ignorance. "But I'm supposed to get your signature. Aunt Glenda said we needed to make sure the inheritance was all figured out. On account of you not having any living relatives and the property might get stuck in probate or something."

Emily looked toward Connor. "What's he trying to say?"

He cut to the venal truth. "He wants you to sign a legal document that would give him possession of the house in Aspen in the case of your death."

Phillip winced. "I didn't want to be blunt about the whole dying thing."

"Yeah, you're a real sensitive guy." Connor didn't know the exact terms of the will but could guess at the provisions that Jamison would have employed. "If Emily had died before she had the deed to the house, I'll bet the property reverted to his estate and, therefore, went to whoever inherited the bulk."

"That's what Jamison would have wanted."

"You can tell Aunt Glenda that the inheritance is safe

from the probate courts. Emily and I intend to update her will. Isn't that right?"

"Absolutely." She beamed a smile at Phillip. "Everything I own goes to my executor, Connor Gallagher."

Phillip stammered, "B-b-but if you don't get the deed transferred, the will won't be valid. Right?"

"Don't you worry," Connor said. "I'll file the paperwork first thing tomorrow morning."

"You can't do that. You can't cheat me out of my property. Forget it." His stumbling confusion turned into rage. Roughly, he shoved Connor's shoulder. "That house is mine. I took care of it for years."

"Wrong again, Philly."

"You can't make me move." He threw a clumsy jab that went wide.

Connor knew better than to retaliate but couldn't stop himself from shoving hard enough to rock Phillip back on his heels. "You'll be lucky if moving out is your only problem."

Phillip sneered. "What's that supposed to mean?"

"It's suspicious," Connor said. "Emily's car is forced off the road. She almost dies. On the very next day, you show up with documentation for what needs to happen if she's dead. It almost seems planned. When did you have those papers drawn up?"

Phillip made a sharp pivot and stalked out the door.

Chapter Eight

The next morning, Emily took an awkward shower, sitting on a chair with her cast wrapped in plastic. An aide washed her hair. A blow-dry was out of the question, which was probably for the best. When she caught sight of her bruised face in the mirror, she figured that no amount of hairstyling was going to make her look cute. The swelling around her eye had faded to dull mauve, and there was a bruise on her jawbone that she hadn't noticed before. Still, she didn't feel too bad—probably a result of pain meds and the pleasure of exchanging her hospital gown for a pair of lightweight pink pajamas that Connor and O'Brien had brought from her house.

Sitting up in the hospital bed, she sipped a cup of herbal tea from the downstairs coffee shop and admired the get-well bouquet of orange daisies and yellow roses from Connor. The man himself sat beside her bed, nursing a cup of coffee. He'd set up his laptop on a table with wheels and was scanning the screen. Though he'd assured her that his office could manage without him for a couple of weeks, she felt guilty for taking him away from work.

"Phillip doesn't seem like the type," she said. "He's a jerk and a spoiled brat. But a murderer? I don't think he's got the nerve."

"It doesn't take courage or smarts to be a stone-cold killer."

"I guess not." She liked the way Connor picked up on her rambling train of thought without reason or explanation. Clearly, they were on the same wavelength.

"Running your car off the road sounds like the kind of dumb plan Phillip would come up with."

She nodded. "True."

"And he has plenty of idiot friends with trucks who he could talk into ramming your car." Connor closed his computer and gave her a smile. "Change of subject. I like your hair."

"You're kidding." She self-consciously tugged at the chin-length bob that would have looked much better if she'd been able to operate a blow-dryer.

"You've got more blond streaks than when you lived in Manhattan. The Colorado sun is good for you."

"It's a healthy lifestyle…if nobody is trying to kill you. Tell me more about Phillip."

He leaned on the railing beside her bed. "He has more to gain than anybody else. With you out of the way, he might get his greedy paws on the house he's been living in, not to mention the furnishings and the artwork."

She scoffed. "What a waste! He knows nothing about art, can't tell a Picasso from a doodle by a second grader."

"Sometimes," Connor said with a wink, "neither can I."

She didn't mean to be snobby, but she'd spent years studying art. It hurt her when true genius wasn't properly appreciated and cared for. While married to Jamison, she'd spent a lot of time and effort curating their art collection and had managed to procure a number of world-famous works. Those works should be shared with people who'd enjoy them. "When all the terms of the will are satisfied, I want to loan several pieces to the Denver Art Museum."

"Phillip will hate that."

"He might change his mind if I can get Aunt Glenda on my side."

"And how are you going to perform that miracle?"

Glenda had hated her from the moment they met. The older woman considered Emily to be common and not worthy of Jamison. However, Glenda would be delighted to promote the Riggs family name. "I'll tell her that the art on loan will have a plaque and be designated as part of the Jamison Riggs collection."

"Excellent plan! If you didn't have that arm in a cast, I'd give you a high five."

Though their buddy-buddy relationship felt comfortable and safe, she wanted more from Connor than high fives and slaps on the back. She tilted her chin toward him and pointed to her cheek. "How about a kiss?"

"Gladly."

When he leaned in close, she turned her head. No doubt, his intention had been to give her a friendly peck, but their lips met. He didn't move away. His mouth pressed firmly against hers, and he deepened the kiss, pushing her lips apart and penetrating with his tongue.

A sizzle spread through her body. She wanted to take it further, but they weren't alone. Beverly stood guard by the door, and she heard people moving and talking in the hallway.

Reluctant to separate from him, her tongue tangled with his. She tasted the slick interior of his mouth. Though their bodies weren't touching, his nearness aroused her. Outer distractions faded into nothingness as she surrendered to the fiery chemistry between them.

A knock on the door interrupted their kiss. Beverly answered, allowing Dr. Fish and two other medical people in white lab coats to enter. After Fish greeted Connor, he gave her a long, steady look and asked, "How are you feeling?"

After that kiss, her blood pressure had to be up. Her heart fluttered. Her breath came in excited little gasps, and she suspected that she was blushing. "I'm good."

"You seem to be tense."

"Not a surprise, considering that my former relatives are trying to kill me." She noticed that Fish's companions exchanged a disbelieving glance. They were probably wondering if they needed to call in a psychiatric consultant. "How are you doing, Fish?"

"A little bird told me that you own an art gallery," he said. "I'd like to buy a piece for my office, something by a local artist."

"I have just the thing. It's from a retired guy who paints incredible landscapes of Grand Lake. We might even be able to talk him into adding a leaping trout."

"Perfect." He introduced the two people who accompanied him. One was studying neurology with Fish.

"And Dr. Lisa Parris is here to take a look at your broken arm, the cracked ribs and the sprained ankle."

"Pleased to meet you, Dr. Parris." When Emily turned in the bed to shake her hand, she experienced a stab of pain from her ribs but forced herself not to wince. "How soon can I get out of the hospital and go home?"

"That depends." With her bouncy ponytail and lack of makeup, Dr. Parris looked so young that even Emily—who was only thirty—wondered about her level of experience. The doctor pushed her glasses up on her nose and said, "Before I can release you, I'll need to look at more X-rays, and you'll have an evaluation from a physical therapist."

"Dr. Parris was a PT for eight years," Fish said. "There's nobody better for getting you back on your feet."

Which was exactly what Emily wanted. "When do we get started?"

"Not so fast." Fish stepped up. "I get first crack."

She listened with half an ear as he rattled off a series of MRIs and scans and so forth that he and his associates would be using on her brain. Glad to be alive, she didn't complain but was anxious to move on. All of this medical effort wouldn't be worth much if someone managed to kill her.

When Fish wrapped up, she said, "If possible, I'd prefer using a wheelchair instead of a gurney to get transferred from one test to the next."

"Shouldn't be a problem," Parris said. "If you'd be

more comfortable, we can move you into this recliner chair right now."

Emily threw off the covers. With the cast, her left arm had limited mobility, and she was grateful for the support from Parris and Fish as she stood. Though the plastic boot protected her sprained ankle, Emily avoided putting weight on it. Hobbling, she made it into the chair where she tried to relax her sore muscles.

After the others departed, she looked up at Connor and let out a sigh. "Everything hurts."

"Should I call the nurse? Get more pain meds?"

"Don't want them." After her time in the induced coma, she was willing to put up with the natural aches and pains. "I'll be okay. It's just that moving around is harder than I thought. The bandages around my ribs are as tight as a corset."

"Can I get you anything?"

"I wish I could wear my blue bathrobe, but there's no way the sleeve will fit over my cast."

"We could cut off the sleeve."

"But I love the robe." She rested her back against the recliner. "It's a shame I can't wear it, especially after you and O'Brien went to so much trouble to get it for me."

"Right." He went across the room to pick up his coffee cup.

"You never told me," she said. "Did you have any trouble getting in?"

"Not a problem. We found the key under the gnome."

When he raised his coffee cup to hide his expression, she had the distinct impression that he wasn't telling her everything. "I guess I should take better care of my home security."

"You need an alarm system," he said. "I already made a note."

She couldn't tell if he was being cagey or if she was too suspicious. "What did you think of my house?"

"It's nice."

Nice? Was that the best description he could come up with? She loved her little two-bedroom cottage. Though the neighborhood was in the middle of the city, the trees around her house—peach, pine and Russian olive—created an aura of privacy. Her garden displayed a bevy of bright pansies and late-blooming roses. She'd replaced two of the front windows with reclaimed stained glass. It was adorable. "Is that all you have to say?"

"I like your giant claw-foot bathtub. Three people could swim laps in there."

Before she could question him further, the physical therapist bounced into the room and ran through a series of exercises Emily could do without leaving the chair or the bed. Working together, they maneuvered her into a wheelchair. And she was whisked away, still wondering if Connor was being evasive.

HE DIDN'T LIKE keeping secrets from her, but Connor feared her reaction to the truth. Late last night when he and O'Brien had entered her house, they found the place ransacked. The only real damage had appeared to be a broken windowpane in the back door where the intruder had reached inside to turn the handle. The details of the search had told a tale to former LAPD detective O'Brien, who had immediately contacted the local police so they could look for fingerprints and other forensic clues.

"But don't get your hopes up," O'Brien had warned him. "Everybody knows enough to wear gloves, and this was a careful, calculated search."

Connor hadn't thought the intruder had been particularly cautious. In the kitchen, plates and glasses had been taken off the shelves. In the upstairs master bedroom, drawers had been pulled open and the contents of the jewelry box dumped on the dresser. "You call this careful?"

"No unnecessary destruction. The intruder wasn't tearing up the place for revenge. And the point of the break-in wasn't burglary. Most of her electronics and jewelry are still here."

"The sparkly stuff in the bedroom is costume jewelry." He knew that Emily had wasted no time in selling the expensive jewelry that Jamison had given her. She hadn't wanted reminders of her marriage. "It's probably not worth much."

In the home office on the first floor, O'Brien had pointed out details. "Here's where the search focused. You got files strewed across the floor. And paintings lifted off the walls, probably looking for a wall safe. Over there on the desk, there's an open space."

"And a hookup for a laptop," he'd said.

"But no computer." O'Brien had paced around the room, being careful not to touch anything. "Here's what I think. The intruder was looking for something small, like a computer flash drive or a code number. Anything come to mind?"

Connor had drawn a blank. "I don't know."

"How about an engagement ring?" O'Brien had asked. "A big shot like Riggs probably spent a small fortune on a giant diamond."

"She doesn't wear it. If she still has it, she probably keeps it in a safe-deposit box."

"That's what I need to hear," O'Brien had announced triumphantly. "A safe-deposit box requires a key and an access code. Who knows what else could be stashed in there? This break-in and search could be about finding that number."

Connor hadn't been convinced last night, and he was equally skeptical this morning. His primary suspects were the Riggs family, and they were too rich to bother with an engagement ring. As for other documents, he was familiar with Emily's business dealings and doubted that she'd been hiding financial secrets from him. Her late, great ex-husband was another story. Jamison had frequently skirted legal boundaries in his investment business.

Outside the hospital X-ray room, Connor and Beverly sat in a waiting area while Emily was treated. He thumbed through a magazine that featured healthy recipes. As usual, Beverly was silent.

Connor cleared his throat. "I should put through a call to O'Brien."

"Suit yourself," Beverly said. "He'll contact us if he has anything to report."

Connor knew that O'Brien was busy with the local cops, checking alibis for Phillip and whoever he had brought with him into town. Maybe Phillip had connected with Kate. Plus, O'Brien would follow up with Sandoval and make sure the rest of the Riggs family had stayed in Aspen last night. "I'm not complaining, but I'm anxious to get results."

Beverly gave a quick nod of acknowledgment.

"O'Brien is doing a good job. So are you." He fidgeted. "I want to take a more active part in the investigation."

She raised her eyebrows and pursed her lips. There was no need for her to speak. He knew what she was implying.

"I know," he said. "I sound like Emily."

"You have your assignment."

It was supposed to be Connor's job to talk to Emily and see if she knew what the intruder had been searching for. He was reluctant, scared that as soon as Emily heard that her cute little house had been broken into, she'd want to go and see for herself. Somehow, he had to discourage her. In the hospital, she was relatively safe.

Beverly stepped away from the waiting area to take a phone call. Her posture was erect, and her movements crisp. Last night, she'd taken a break, using another bodyguard to fill in for her, so she wouldn't get too tired to do her job. When she returned and sat beside him, she said, "You have to tell her about the intruder. The cops are almost done, and TST Security is standing by. We're ready to install the new locks and a top-of-the-line alarm system, but we've got a problem. Either we replace the back door or repair it. That should be Emily's decision."

"I meant to tell her first thing this morning."

"But you didn't."

"As soon as she hears about somebody breaking into her house, she'll bust out of the hospital. There'll be no stopping her."

"That's what I'd do," Beverly said. "A break-in is personal. It's a violation."

Beverly was a former gunnery sergeant in the Marine Corps. She could take care of herself, but Emily was vulnerable, untrained in self-defense. "What if the killer is waiting for her to show up? Even if her doctors agree to release her, it's not safe."

"It's unlikely for the intruder to hang around while the cops are there," Beverly said. "But I agree with you. Less exposure is better."

He was glad they were on the same page. T. J. Beverly was careful to maintain a cool, professional distance, but Connor sensed a budding friendship between them. "Are you any closer to getting me a gun? If the intruder had been at the house last night, I could have used a weapon."

"It's not going to happen, Connor. The best I can do for you is a stun gun."

"I'm okay with that."

Any advice he could get when it came to protecting himself and Emily was welcome. Though he didn't have formal training in self-defense and never went looking for trouble, he'd grown up in a tough neighborhood. Other guys told him that he was a good man to have on your side in a barroom brawl.

"A suggestion," Beverly said. "Tell Emily what's going on with her house as soon as you get a chance. Otherwise, she'll never trust you."

"I'm not sure how much she trusts me now."

She hadn't hesitated to sign over the authority to make life-and-death medical decisions for her, but he didn't think she'd blindly trust him to pick out a new door for her house. During the months when she'd talked to him about her disintegrating marriage, she'd listened to his opinions but had done whatever the hell she wanted. The moment when he really felt her lack of confidence in his advice came when he offered her a place to stay in New York, namely in the guest room at his apartment. Instead, she'd packed up and moved to Denver.

When Emily was wheeled out of the X-ray room, Connor and Beverly trailed her through the corridors to her room. He mentally rehearsed what he was going to say to her about the intruder. Gradually, he'd reveal what had happened. He'd hold her hand. Maybe he ought to arrange for lunch to be delivered. She was easier to handle when her belly was full.

In her room, Special Agent Wellborn was waiting. He'd changed from jeans into a suit and tie but still wore the crocodile cowboy boots. The guy was a Manhattan fashionista, but his posture and bearing echoed Beverly's style. There was a mutual respect and recognition, almost as though they were wearing uniforms. When they shook hands, he saw the bond between them.

Wellborn approached Emily in her wheelchair. "It's nice to actually meet you. The last time I was in your hospital room, we weren't formally introduced."

"You're with the FBI, right?"

"Yes."

"You were part of the investigation into my ex-husband's death."

Connor heard the edginess in her tone. Though she was obviously tired, with her shoulders slumped and her hands folded listlessly in her lap, she wasn't ready to accept her exhaustion and sleep.

Politely, Wellborn answered, "I'm with the White-Collar Crime Unit. We looked into the death of Jamison Riggs."

"You questioned me," she said.

"Yes."

"And I talked to one of your colleagues on the phone," she said. "He drew a couple of obvious conclusions. Number one was that I hadn't spent any time with my ex-husband in months and didn't have the opportunity to poison him—if, in fact, he was poisoned. Number two, I wasn't in love with him anymore."

They were entering dangerous emotional territory, and Connor wanted to warn Wellborn to tread lightly, but there was no need. This federal agent was smooth.

"I wish I'd had the opportunity to interview you in depth. Working together, we might have come to more useful deductions. I'm inclined to believe the attacks on you are connected to Jamison's death. I believe you've spoken to Kate Sylvester."

"I have."

"Are you feeling well enough to talk about what happened at your house?"

She sat up a bit straighter in her wheelchair. "My house?"

"The intruder was searching for something small,"

Wellborn said. "Do you have any idea what he or she was after?"

"Intruder?" She turned her head and glared at Connor. "You knew about this."

"Yes."

Flames shot from her eyes and charbroiled the well-meaning excuses he'd been prepared to offer. His motivations had been good: he hadn't wanted her to get excited, demand to be involved and put herself in harm's way. His intention had been to protect her.

At the moment, he felt he was the one who needed protection...*from* her.

Chapter Nine

Outrage exploded her exhaustion and weakness. Emily forgot about the twinge in her ankle and the aching from her bruised ribs. Still staring at Connor, she asked, "Was there a lot of damage to my house?"

"According to O'Brien, it was a careful search. The intruder didn't tear your place apart seeking revenge."

"Doesn't make me feel better," she growled.

"A pane of glass in the back door was broken, and it looks like your laptop might have been stolen."

"But you don't really know," she said, "because you're not familiar with the stuff in my house. Maybe I had a million-dollar sculpture on the table in the entry. And what if I had a cat, a sweet little calico cat named Taffy? What if the intruder kicked Taffy and she was hiding under the house, meowing in pain?"

"I didn't see any food bowls or litter boxes."

"Because I don't have a cat." She wished she hadn't hopped down this rabbit hole, but she was making a point. "Bottom line, I'm the only one who can give a true inventory of what was in my house, whether it was a cat or valuable artwork."

"You're right."

"I can't believe you didn't tell me right away."

"A mistake," he said. "I apologize."

Adrenaline fueled her anger, but she knew better than to unleash her unbridled fury on Connor. He'd meant her no harm. The opposite, in fact. He had been trying to do the right thing. The warmth in his eyes deflected her rage, and she reminded herself that this wasn't his fault. She muttered, "It's all right."

"I didn't hear you."

"You're forgiven, okay? And for your information, my laptop wasn't stolen. I took it with me to Aspen. The poor thing was probably smashed to bits in the crash. Let's move on." She stared at the FBI agent, who looked like he'd stepped from the pages of a men's fashion mag. "How can I help your investigation?"

"This might be a long conversation," he said. "Would you like to lie down?"

Being in bed seemed like a position of weakness, and she wanted to appear strong so she'd be taken seriously. Her powder puff–pink jammies put her at a definite disadvantage when compared to Wellborn's designer clothes. "I'd rather sit in the chair. Also, I'd like more tea. And I think I ordered a sandwich."

In moments, her demands were met. One of the aides provided a light blanket to cover her lap. Someone found a pot of hot water for tea and a container of ice water with a bendy straw. A freshly made turkey sandwich she'd ordered for lunch from the hospital kitchen appeared before her, which meant it must be noon. Already? She was anxious to get moving, ready for action.

In one sense, the break-in at her house was good news. Local law enforcement had a whole new area to search for clues. In the crime-solving shows on television, a single hair or a fiber could be used to identify and track the criminal, but she couldn't count on forensics. Lots of people—including local artists and workmen—came into and out of her house, and all of them left traces behind. Unless they found something that pointed to the Riggs family or some other direct suspect, the best kind of clue would be if the intruder had stolen something significant. And the only way they'd find out about such a theft was for her to go to the house and look around.

Before she started her talk with Wellborn, Dr. Parris interrupted. She had good news. After a consult with a podiatrist, Emily's ankle injury was downgraded to a light sprain, which meant she'd be up and around, possibly using a cane, in a few days. Also, her arm cast could be replaced with a smaller one.

"From wrist to elbow," Parris said. "I don't know why the ER doctors put on such a giant cast in the first place."

Emily had many other doubts about the hospital team led by Dr. Thorson, but she didn't criticize. Thorson sounded like a jerk, but the surgeons in Aspen had saved her life when she'd flatlined on the operating table. "I have only one question. When can I go home?"

"Dr. Troutman has the final say," Parris said. "As far as I'm concerned, you can go tomorrow if you have someone to take care of you."

Connor spoke up. "I can have your house cleaned before that."

"I'd rather you didn't," Wellborn said. "I'd like Emily to walk through and see if she notices anything unusual."

"I'd like that, too," she said. "A walk-through would be great. Can I do that this afternoon, Dr. Parris?"

"I wouldn't advise walking on that ankle," the doctor said, "but you could take a field trip in a wheelchair if Dr. Troutman gives the okay."

Emily's spirits lifted. Finally, she'd be involved, taking charge of her own life. Beaming a smile, she turned to Wellborn. "You said the intruder was looking for something small. Do you have an idea of what that might be?"

"A flash drive, a ring, a key," he said, listing possibilities. "Do you have a safe-deposit box?"

"Yes, it's for documents like the loan papers for my house, my car title and stuff like that. Nothing of value to anybody else."

"Jewelry?"

"Diamond earrings from my mother, a couple of gold chains." She concentrated, trying to envision what was in there. And then she blushed. There was an encouraging card that Connor had sent when her divorce was final. He'd signed with *I love you*, and she remembered reading it again and again, rubbing her thumb across the print and telling herself that she was making too much of a casual sign-off. "There's a smaller box inside, filled with mementos, and a notebook with a list of my passwords."

"Do I have your permission to access the box?"

"I'd like to come along when you do." She was reluctant to allow unrestricted access to her personal possessions. It was bad enough that the police were at her house, poking around her things. "What if the intruder already found the key? It's not really hidden. I keep it in my jewelry box."

"Give me the name of your bank," Wellborn said. "We'll put a Stop and Seize on anyone attempting to impersonate you."

While he dealt with the bureaucratic issues, she sank back in the recliner and nibbled at the edges of her turkey sandwich. When she mentally reviewed the contents of her house, she wasn't aware of anything that merited breaking and entering. Her home wasn't a showplace like the massive house she and Jamison had furnished in Aspen, and she wasn't a secretive person. Jamison had been a hundred times more enigmatic than she, and he continued to surprise her from the grave. Never did she think he'd leave that beautiful house to her. And the art!

The idea of seeing those paintings and sculptures again gave her chills: the small Renoir of a girl on a swing, a couple of wry lithographs by Banksy, a Georgia O'Keeffe calla lily and so much more. One of her big regrets in the divorce was losing access to these wonderful artworks. By the end, she'd been ready to give up almost anything. Not that she hated Jamison, but she desperately wanted her marriage to be over.

Connor pulled a plastic chair up beside her. "Do you really feel well enough to go to the house?"

She nodded. "And I'd appreciate if you'd back me up with Fish."

"I'm not in love with the idea, but I understand why you want to go. We'll make sure you're well guarded."

She reached toward him and was glad when he clasped her hand in his familiar grasp. Forgiveness went both ways. "I'm willing to cooperate, Connor, but you've got to keep me in the loop and let me make my own decisions."

"Done."

"As soon as possible, I want to go to my gallery in the art district," she said. "I'm not too worried about a break-in there. I've got decorative iron grillwork on the doors and windows, plus a security alarm that screams for twenty minutes and calls the cops."

"Do you need to be open for business?"

"I wish!" She grinned. "It's not a problem if I'm closed for a couple of days. I don't get a lot of walk-in traffic. Most of my sales come from personal contacts and from showings. I have an event scheduled for next week."

"A wine-and-cheese thing," he said in a world-weary tone that indicated he'd attended too many of those *things*.

"Get your mind out of Manhattan," she said. "This showing is all about Southwestern art and sculpture. We're having chips, salsa, tequila and a mariachi band."

"I'm in."

Wellborn rejoined them. "Your safe-deposit box is secure. If anyone tries to use the key, they'll be detained."

"Thank you." She nodded her approval. "I'd probably have my own problems with the bank if I tried to access my accounts. I've got no ID. My handbag and wallet went flying out of the car when I crashed."

Wellborn placed his briefcase on the foot of the hospital bed, flipped it open and took out her bronze leather purse, which was much battered but still intact. "Deputy Sandoval found this when they were hauling the remains of your car up the cliff. Also, here are your keys."

"My phone?"

"They didn't find it. That's treacherous terrain."

"I'm glad to have my handbag." She was gradually reassembling the shattered pieces of her life. Shoving the remains of her sandwich out of the way, she unfastened the clasp on her purse. Inside was her wallet with her driver's license, an insurance card, credit cards and twenty-seven dollars in cash. The contents were so pleasantly normal that she wanted to cheer.

"Before we get started," Wellborn said, "do you have questions for me?"

"I do," Connor said. "How much can you tell us about the people in Aspen? We know Phillip is in Denver. What about the others?"

"Patricia and Glenda admit to nothing and have pretty much barred the door. The family attorney refuses to allow law enforcement to enter any of their homes without a search warrant, and we don't have enough evidence to get a judge to sign off."

"Technically," Connor said, "the house that Jamison owned now belongs to Emily. As soon as I have the deeds and paperwork filed, she can open the door to a search."

"I'd appreciate it," Wellborn said.

"What about Thorson?" Connor asked.

"The doctor is taking three months' unpaid leave while the hospital administration decides what to do about him. They aren't real happy after the incident with the ambulance."

Until now, Beverly had been standing quietly near the door. She cleared her throat. "This incident, can you tell me about it?"

"No big deal." Aware that he'd behaved badly, Connor tried to wave it away. "Thorson and the Riggs family attempted to abduct Emily—who was unconscious—and we stopped them."

"You're leaving something out," Wellborn said. "If we'd followed the rules, Thorson would have been fired. The administration extended leniency because they doubted you'd sue after you'd been so aggressive."

"They deserved worse."

"You tried to grab my gun."

"Not good," Beverly said. "You are so not getting a weapon."

"Fine," Connor said. "Let's get back to the subject. What else is going on with Thorson?"

"Patricia is angry with him, threatened to kick him out of her life."

Though Emily had been in a coma through most of the ambulance drama, she was glad Thorson was being punished. "He's still in Aspen, right?"

"He was at his apartment last night," Wellborn said.

"The only person of interest whose whereabouts were unaccounted for during the time of the break-in is Kate Sylvester. From what I understand, you talked to her before the reading of the will."

"That's right. And Connor said he saw her when we first arrived at the hospital."

"I think so," he said, "but I don't really know the woman."

Agent Wellborn glanced between them, reading their expressions. His features were arranged in a professionally neutral expression, neither happy nor sad nor enthusiastic. But she had the impression that Kate's appearance in Denver was significant to his investigation. She asked, "Have you interviewed Kate before?"

"Extensively," he said. "She was close to Jamison, both professionally and in other ways."

"That's putting it nicely," she said. "At the investment firm, she had seniority over him. In their personal relationship she worked under him. Or maybe not. She strikes me as a woman who likes to be on the top."

"I want you to tell us—in detail—about your conversation with her. Don't leave anything out."

Emily inhaled a deep breath, then exhaled and started talking. "I ran into her after I left the downstairs restroom at Patricia's chalet, which is a crazy-opulent room with tons of marble and gleaming gold tiles. A little excessive in my opinion. I mean, what kind of person needs all that glitter and shimmer to go to the bathroom? Anyway, I went down the hall from the bathroom and ducked into a library. Kate followed me in."

She vividly remembered the moment when she recognized the stunning auburn-haired woman who'd slept with her husband before he was an ex-husband. Emily wasn't one for slut shaming, and she had struggled to find the politically correct words to let Kate know that her behavior was despicable. Before she could unleash her tirade, Kate had said, "He dumped me, too."

That simple statement gave Emily a burst of smug pleasure because she was the one who had dumped Jamison and not the other way around. Sure, he'd had an affair with Kate, but Emily was the dumper. He was the dumpee.

Emily shot a glance toward Connor. "Kate thinks we have something in common, but I don't. Apart from both of us having had sex with the same man, we're very different."

"How so?" Wellborn asked.

"I'm into art. She's into numbers. We both have good taste, but she goes for the classics and I like to try new things. As far as I can tell, she has zero sense of humor. Oh, and she's way more competitive than I am. With her Wall Street job, I guess she needs to be fierce and ambitious."

"Was this the first time you talked with her?" Wellborn asked.

"We'd met at company dinners and work-related events, but we were usually part of a group. She's not the type of woman who hangs out with female friends."

"Why do you think she sought you out?"

"At first, I thought she wanted to talk about Jamison. Being in Aspen reminded me of him and the good times we'd had. He loved the mountains."

And he'd died too young. His death saddened her. In spite of their divorce and their final angry arguments, he held a place in her heart that no one else would ever fill. It felt like she'd never mourned him, that she didn't have the right to that sorrow.

Connor squeezed her hand and whispered, "Are you okay?"

"I'm sorry he's gone."

"Me, too."

She turned toward Wellborn. "Kate said something about how nobody knew Jamison better than the two of us—the ex-wife and the ex-girlfriend."

"Do you agree with that?" Wellborn asked.

"We both knew him well, but he was different with Kate." She glanced over at Connor. "You know what I mean, don't you? Kate was a good match for the man he had become. They were both consumed by their work. I'm surprised they had time for, um, anything else."

Wellborn pointed her back toward her conversation with Kate before the reading. "What else did she talk to you about?"

"She wanted to compare memories of Jamison. Where had we gone to dinner? Who did we go on double dates with? What kind of gifts did he give me for Valentine's Day? She wanted to make it a competition where he gave her better gifts and introduced her to more important people. Kate is the kind of person who goes to an art gallery and takes selfies next to the paintings rather than actually looking at them. She creeps me out."

Emily remembered the uncomfortable sensation

when Kate had started adding up their time on vacation. The red-haired woman seemed to have a calculator for a brain. "And then she switched gears and wanted to be my friend. She offered to come to my house and check out anything Jamison might have given me to see if it was valuable."

"Such as?"

"She talked about a portfolio, investments and a secret bank account." Emily raised an eyebrow, giving Wellborn a meaningful look. "Interested?"

"I am," he said. "Did she mention specific names of companies and investments?"

"I don't remember. The whole situation—Jamison's death, being at Patricia's home, the woman who slept with my husband acting like we should be besties—it was all so surreal. If I'd known what was to come, I'd have committed every single word to memory." Emily shook her head. "But she kept stressing that I might not be aware of how much Jamison's financial gifts were really worth."

"Ironic," Connor said. "A few minutes later, Emily learned that Jamison had bequeathed her the Aspen house, complete with furniture and art—a multimillion-dollar gift that outstripped anything he'd ever gifted to Kate."

"And she's real familiar with the house," Emily said. "She told me that she was staying there with Phillip. That's why she was at the will reading in the first place."

Wellborn held up his hand, signaling a halt. "Are you saying that Kate Sylvester and Phillip Riggs are close?"

"They aren't lovers if that's what you mean. At least,

I don't think they are. Who knows? They hang out to-gether, go to the same places, see the same people." She shrugged. "That whole bunch—the family and Jamison's friends—are as thick as thieves."

"An apt comparison," Wellborn said. "What did Jamison leave to Kate?"

"A designer briefcase and a Rolex."

"Versus a house in Aspen," Wellborn said. "I'd say you won the competition for best gift from Jamison."

That wasn't a game Emily wanted to play. If she'd married Jamison for his money, they would still be together. Something more important had been lost—their love.

Chapter Ten

Tucked into her wheelchair and dressed in loose-fitting lavender sweats with the left arm slashed open to accommodate her cast, Emily gazed through the windows of the ambulance van at the late-afternoon sunlight. She loved autumn. In the mountains, the foliage had already turned, but in town the process was belated. Only a few of the trees showed their September colors of orange, gold and scarlet. She inhaled a deep breath. Even in traffic, the air smelled crisp. She was glad to be out, so glad to be alive.

The main reason Fish had agreed to let her leave the hospital to check out the ransacking at her house was that Special Agent in Charge Jaiden Wellborn had told him that her observations might aid a federal investigation. An outstanding negotiator, SAC Wellborn radiated authority but was also respectful to the doctor. And it helped that her brain scans were positive. No doubt Fish would have insisted that she stay on bed rest if she hadn't been on the mend.

Ever since she'd got to the hospital, they'd been running tests, scans and MRIs. Fish and the other neurologists hadn't been able to pinpoint the cause of her seizure. Though there was still a bit of swelling, they hadn't found clots, tumors or other brain damage. Fish diagnosed her with a simple concussion resulting from a blow to the head. Also, he'd suggested that her seizure might have been due to exposure to a poison or an allergic reaction, and he had ordered tox screens along with other blood tests.

Poison? Was it coincidence that Connor had seen Kate moments before she went into anaphylactic shock? It seemed impossible that Kate would attempt to poison her in a hospital with so many witnesses, but stranger things had happened. Nobody had believed that a healthy, young man like Jamison had contracted a mysterious illness and died at the height of his career.

Emily added attempted poisoning to the list of murderous attacks. First, there was the truck forcing her off the road, and then her IV bag had been switched on the flight from Denver, and now she might have been poisoned. She was using up her good luck faster than a cat runs through nine lives.

In the back of the van with her, Connor asked Beverly when she could get him a stun gun that wouldn't require a special permit. She told him that there was no reason for him to have a weapon while she was on duty.

"Let me do my job," she said.

"I can be your backup."

"To chase down ambulance drivers?" She'd obviously taken note of the incident when Connor had been ready to shoot first and ask questions later.

"Here's an idea," Emily piped up. "Connor can use my Beretta M9."

They both turned toward her, gaping like a couple of surprised goldfish. Beverly spoke first. "Where do you keep your weapon?"

"It's locked in a metal box in the back of my closet, along with a half dozen other boxes. I should have mentioned it to Wellborn, but I didn't think of it. I hardly ever take the Beretta out of the box."

"Are you trained to use the gun?" Beverly asked.

"Absolutely." After her parents passed away, her uncle had given her the Beretta when she was sixteen. His reasoning had been that if she was capable of protecting herself, he could leave her alone for long periods of time. He'd thought it was a really nice present, which said a lot about his fitness as a father figure. He was her mother's brother and shared her fondness for booze. Also, he got a kick out of teaching her how to handle the weapon. "I know how to lock and load, how to clean the M9, how to take it apart and how to aim."

"Have you ever shot anything?" Beverly asked.

"Nothing human."

Connor finally closed his gaping mouth. "Why didn't I know about the Beretta?"

"It's not a big deal. Do I have to remind you that I grew up in Colorado?" She gave him a smile as she pointed through the side window. "This is the corner to my street."

"Nice neighborhood," Connor said. "Quiet."

In this older part of town, the trees were tall and well established, the houses were brick and the design of the homes varied from three-story Tudor houses to cozy cottages like hers, which was set back a long way from the front sidewalk. A driveway extended all the way to the garage in the back, and it was filled by two police vehicles parked end to end. The medical van squeezed in behind the DPD police cruiser and the driver came around to the side so he could operate the lift for her wheelchair.

"I don't really need that," she said. "I can stand on my good leg and hop."

"Use the lift," Connor and Beverly said in unison. At least they agreed on something.

Grumbling, she stayed in the chair and descended from the van on a square platform operated by hydraulics. The real problem would come when they got to her side door. Two steep stairs led to the porch, and there wasn't a ramp. An even bigger problem: her bedroom was on the second floor. With the driver and Beverly accompanying them, Connor pushed her chair along the edge of the driveway past three peach trees.

"Stop," she ordered.

He halted so quickly that she almost spilled forward. "What's up?"

"I want a peach." She pointed to the branches where luscious, ripe fruit dangled beyond her reach. The season was almost over. Leaves on the tree were tinged with yellow.

He reached up and picked two. "One for you and one for me."

As she rubbed her thumb over the peach fuzz, she wished they'd been visiting her home under different circumstances. "Let's go around to the back so I can see the broken door."

He rounded the corner and went between the house and the garage, where he parked her wheelchair on a small concrete patio. Four lawn chairs circled a glass-topped table, and there was a comfortable chaise with a striped cushion. A long low redwood box held a display of petunias and pansies in varying shades of pink, yellow and purple. The landscaping—with all the trees—had been one of the features that had sold her on this house. She liked the shrubs along the back fence and the climbing red roses on two arched trellises.

"It's nice out here," he said. "You aren't going to be happy about what you find inside the house."

"I know." She realized that she'd come into the garden to avoid the moment when she had to confront the reality of having had an intruder. "I love this house. It's the first place where I've lived alone."

Growing up, she'd been with her parents, of course. When they died, she lived with her uncle. In college and her first years working in New York she'd needed roommates to help pay the rent. Then she'd been married.

"Do you miss having other people around?" he asked.

"Not a bit."

"I know what you mean," he said. "When I finally got my own place, I loved the peace and quiet. My mom said I'd get bored."

"Did you?"

"Not yet," he said. "I love my big, loud family, but sometimes I wish I'd moved farther away from Brooklyn."

"Could you ever go back to living with someone else?"

"That depends on the someone."

Sensing a change in the atmosphere between them, she looked up into his chocolate-brown eyes and saw an enticing heat. When he mentioned living with *someone*, he wasn't referring to a new roommate or family member who needed a place to stay. Connor was taking a frank look at his life and considering a major life change—having a girlfriend move in with him to share his home and his life. At least, she hoped that was what he'd been thinking.

Though they'd never been anything more than friends, the chemistry had been bubbling between them ever since her divorce. She asked, "Are you looking for this *someone*?"

Inside her head, she chanted, *Pick me, pick me, pick me.*

"I'm not ruling out any possibilities, except for not dating anybody I work with. There are blind dates and online dating. Maybe I'll see someone on the street. Or maybe I've already met someone and don't know it yet." Quickly, he changed the subject. "You know, Emily, you don't have to go inside the house. We can return to the van right now. I'll arrange for somebody to come in and clean up the mess. And when you come home, your house will look like it's supposed to."

His offer was tempting, but she'd spent most of her life avoiding conflicts and having other people solve her problems. Maybe Kate had been correct when she'd said that Emily didn't understand what she'd had and what she'd lost. "I have to do this for myself. I'm ready."

He wheeled her to the concrete stairs leading to the

back door with the busted window. "There are two ways we can get you up the stairs. The driver and I can lift the chair or I can carry you. Your choice."

"Let's do a carry," she said. "It can be practice for hiking up the staircase to the second floor."

"And we need to go there because…"

"My bedroom is upstairs."

"And?"

"It's where I keep my Beretta."

As soon as she rose from the wheelchair, he scooped her into his arms and cradled her against his chest. Her good arm was closest to his body, and she slipped her hand up and around his neck. Her intention had been to make it easier to carry her. The effect was different—warm, sensual and intimate.

She'd known Connor for years, which meant plenty of hugs and casual physical contact. Once or twice, they'd danced together. Other than the few kisses they'd shared, nothing had felt as extraordinary and personal as this moment. Though they were surrounded by other people—the ambulance driver, Beverly, uniformed officers and forensic technicians—it seemed like they existed in a bubble that was their own special world.

She jostled against him. Two layers of fabric separated them: her velour sweatshirt and his black V-neck cashmere sweater. And yet their touch started a friction that thrilled her. *Was it possible for her to hear his heartbeat, or was she imagining the steady, strong thump?* Despite her injuries, she couldn't help responding to his nearness. If she'd been able to read her reaction on a brain scan, Emily knew that her pleasure centers would be blazing. She was utterly, totally, happily aware of him as a man.

Inside the house when he returned her to the wheelchair, the real world came back into sharp focus. One of the CSI investigators offered a pair of latex gloves, Emily turned him down. Her fingerprints would be all over her house. The others had to wear plastic bootees to cover their shoes. This space wasn't her home anymore. It was a crime scene.

Her charming kitchen looked like it had been taken over by an army of destructive raccoons. Drawers hung open. Shelves had been emptied. Her cute retro canisters for flour, sugar, coffee and tea had been overturned and the contents were spread across the polished granite countertop.

"Seriously," she muttered, "did they think I'd hide my valuables in a sugar jar?"

"You'd be surprised," Wellborn said. "People stash things behind the sink, inside the light fixtures and in the freezer."

She glanced at her fridge, noting that the contents were strewed across the floor. An unpleasant smell emanated from a container of leftover *moo shu* pork. "Not much real food in there. I was a New Yorker so long that I picked up the bad habit of grabbing takeout rather than cooking."

Accompanied by her little entourage, she wheeled from the kitchen to the front room. The afternoon light shone multicolored through the two stained glass windows onto a scene of clutter, which, thankfully, didn't show much permanent damage. A chair was overturned but not broken. The intruder had yanked the pillows off the sofa but hadn't torn them apart. Several books had been pulled from the built-in shelves and flipped through. *Smart move*, she thought. A lot of people hid things in hollowed-out books; she wasn't one of them.

"He didn't touch my flat-screen TV," she said. "Does that mean the intruder isn't a burglar?"

"I'm going to say yes." Wellborn strolled around the room with his hands in his trouser pockets. "This search seems to be targeted to a specific item. Are you getting any ideas about what they were looking for?"

"Not really."

They made quick work of the downstairs closets and bathroom. Her small office had taken the worst hit. Files were scattered like a manila leaf storm. The contents were personal and mostly outdated because she kept track of her bills on her computer. "I'm glad I keep all the invoices, receipts and consignment papers for my business at the gallery. I wouldn't want an intruder to have access to that information."

"What's going on over here?" Connor gestured toward the blank wall between the door and the closet. "It's not like you to leave an open space."

She visualized the way the wall had looked last week: a plain white background for three sharp graphic prints in black and white. "I had simple art so I wouldn't be distracted when I sat at the desk. The intruder must have taken it down looking for a wall safe."

"Do you have a wall safe?" Wellborn asked.

"I didn't think I needed one. There's a fireproof vault at my gallery."

The usually clean surface of her desk was cluttered with the contents of the drawers. Carefully, she picked through the array of pens, notepads, paper clips, business cards, rulers and scissors. "I can't say for sure, but I think I'm missing a couple of flash drives. And I don't see the spare keys for my house and my car."

"You won't need the house keys," Connor said.

"Or the keys for my poor, dead Hyundai."

"You'll have new locks. The people Beverly works for are upgrading your security. As soon as the CSI people are done and you choose the style of door you want to replace the one that got busted, they can get started."

"What about keys for your gallery?" Wellborn asked.

"I use a secure keypad."

"You might consider the same treatment for your home."

The need to turn her charming little cottage into a fortress angered her, but she couldn't hide behind rose-colored glasses and pretend nothing was wrong. Some-body was trying to kill her. "I wish I could find some more useful clues."

"Try to put yourself in Kate's position," Wellborn suggested. "What would she want? It might possibly be an object that belonged to your ex-husband."

What would a woman like Kate really want? Emily didn't think her foe valued a sentimental treasure or a thing of beauty. She wanted power, and the route she'd chosen was through money.

At the staircase, they decided that she and Connor would be the first to go up to the second floor, and the others would follow. Unlike the first time he had lifted her, there was an awkward pause before she tumbled into his arms. They'd both been somewhat aroused and neither of them wanted to look foolish. As he maneuvered to pick her up, her movements were as floppy as a rag doll.

But when he held her against his chest, nothing else mattered. She didn't care how she'd got into the position but was happy to be there. Tilting her head, she looked up at him. They were so close. Her breath mingled with his.

"Hang on," he said. "I don't want to bump you against the wall."

She wouldn't have minded too much. What was one more bump? But she welcomed the invitation to tighten her grasp around his neck. To keep her arm cast from dangling, she angled her left wrist across her belly and turned her body toward him. As he climbed the staircase, her breast rubbed against him, and the pressure aroused sensations she hadn't experienced in quite a while. He smelled clean and fresh like sandalwood soap. In the V-neck of his sweater, she glimpsed a sexy tuft of hair that made her want to plunge her hand inside and caress his muscular chest. The black cashmere was unbelievably soft against her cheek. Giving a small moan of satisfaction, she burrowed into the hollow below his chin.

At the top of the stairs, they were nearly alone. Everybody else was on the first floor.

"We made it." She gazed up at him. "My bedroom is on the right."

Leaning down, he kissed her forehead. "I wish we had something more suggestive planned for your bedroom."

"Not yet."

"But soon," he promised as he carried her into the bedroom and set her down on the bed, where the white duvet had been tossed aside, revealing smooth lavender sheets. He lingered, and she thought he might kiss her again, but then everybody else piled into her bedroom.

Connor stood up straight. "Let's take care of first things first. Where's your Beretta?"

"It's inside a Doc Martens shoebox at the back of my closet."

"If it's there," Connor said. "I can't believe the intruder would leave a weapon behind."

Her gaze flicked around the cozy bedroom with blond Swedish modern furniture and accents of purple and yellow. Apart from some of her clothing that had been tossed around, the biggest mess was on top of the dresser, where her jewelry box had been dumped. From where she sat on the edge of her bed, she could see the sparkle and shine. None of her costume jewelry was worth more than a couple hundred bucks, but she liked each piece, and she hated that a stranger had been touching them, rifling through her house, invading her privacy.

She looked away from the dresser. The wall opposite her bed was decorated with dozens of snapshots of places and people who were special to her, ranging from coffee with friends to the house in Aspen to the most beautiful sunset she'd ever witnessed. This wall hadn't received the same treatment as the one in her office downstairs;

none of these photos were large enough to hide a wall safe. Still, as she gazed, she noticed that a couple of the snapshots were askew, and the pattern she'd arranged them in was unbalanced.

One was missing.

Chapter Eleven

Connor emerged from the closet, shoebox in hand. Unlike the kitchen and the office, the clutter in the bedroom wasn't too bad, and the closet—where dozens of shoeboxes were stacked—looked like it had barely been touched. He placed the box labeled Doc Martens on the bed beside her and lifted the lid. Inside was the locked metal container that held her Beretta M9.

"Not the first place I'd go looking," he said, "but if I was searching, I might dig through the boxes. I'm surprised the intruder didn't discover the gun."

"I think I know why," Emily said. "By the time the intruder got to the closet, she'd already found what she was looking for."

"*She?* As in Kate Sylvester?"

"I'm afraid so."

Emily had everybody's attention—Wellborn, Beverly, the ambulance driver and two plainclothes officers. "Explain," Connor said.

"When Kate and I were talking in Aspen, she mentioned Jamison's habit of leaving cute little personal notes on the backs of photographs."

"He did that when we were in college," Connor said. "He'd take a photo on a first date, make a note and send it to his latest girlfriend. Women thought it was sweet."

"Jamison was good at courtship. In the long term? Not so much." She pointed to the wall opposite her bed, where twenty or more framed snapshots were clustered in groups. "Tell me what you see."

The first thing he noticed was that his smiling face appeared in two photos: a group shot on a ski slope in Aspen and a touristy pose on a bridge in Central Park. He recognized several other people: friends in New York, people she'd worked with and artists whose work she'd displayed. Noticeably absent were photos of family events, like birthdays or Christmas. Emily had no siblings and her relationship with her uncle wasn't something she talked about. Her in-laws and Jamison had also been deleted from her life.

"Do you get it?" she asked. "Anything odd?"

Connor studied the photos more intently, trying to decipher her meaning. He figured that Emily had taken most of these pictures, and the composition showed her natural artistic sensibility in terms of balance and light. Each shot captured a glimpse into the character of the subject, whether it was beauty, humor, joy or poignant sadness.

Beverly was the one who spotted the anomaly. "This group of three photos on the far end seems lopsided. Was something removed?"

"There was a fourth picture," Emily said. "It was a friend of mine feeding a banana to a blue iguana."

"In the Cayman Islands," Connor said. He remembered that group trip very well, especially the sunrise morning when he and Emily had got up early and walked along the beach. "Your friend Liz Perry was fascinated by the iguanas and earned herself the nickname of *Lizzie Lizard*."

"The Caymans," Wellborn said. "I have a bad idea about where this is headed."

"While we were there," Emily said, "Jamison had me open an account in this strange little bank with a small lobby and a floor-to-ceiling safe. I signed a bunch of documents and let them take my photo and fingerprints. It wasn't the first time Jamison guided me through a business transaction."

"I advised you not to sign anything without letting me review it first." Connor hadn't wanted her husband to take advantage of her easygoing nature. "I was right there. On the island. You could have called me over."

"Jamison gave me a logical reason for setting up the account, and I believed him. He was my husband." Her voice quavered, but she held her emotions in check. "He kept the account number, and I didn't really think about it again."

"And Jamison didn't mention this account in the divorce proceedings." He figured they were onto something. Jamison had a mysterious stash in the Caymans.

"Like Kate said, I don't pay much attention when it comes to financial dealings. And by the time our marriage ended, I was more concerned with getting out than finances."

Her self-critical tone bothered him. He wanted to tell her that she had nothing to be ashamed about. Her mistake hadn't been careless or stupid. The reason Emily slipped up was that she'd trusted the wrong man.

Wellborn asked, "Can you give me the name of the bank?"

"I don't remember. There can't be many."

"Actually, there are," he said. "Offshore banking is a big business, and there are well over a hundred institutions in the islands. Did Jamison use your name to open the account?"

"My hyphenated name—*Benton-Riggs*."

Her account would be filed under *B*, distancing her from her husband in case the White-Collar Crimes Unit managed to get a peek inside the records of this unnamed, offshore bank. This investigation would be complicated and might not yield results.

SAC Wellborn appeared to be up for the challenge. He whipped his phone from his pocket, ready to call in the reinforcements—CPA investigators armed with actuarial tables and calculators. "Is there anything else you can tell me, Emily?"

"There's a reason that Kate took the photo." Twin frown lines appeared between her eyebrows. "There were numbers scrawled across the back. Jamison must have written them."

"What kind of numbers?"

"I thought it was an international phone number, but it could have been a bank account. Jamison was always scrawling numbers, notes, whatever on anything he could find. I really didn't think much of it." She shook her head. "It's amazing how an attempt on your life changes the way you see things. If Kate has that number, will she have access to whatever is in there?"

"Not immediately," Wellborn said. "You usually need the account number and a password or code. Do you remember a password?"

"I think I typed something into a keypad. Who knows what it was? I've got dozens of passwords, ranging from a yogurt store to my retirement account." Clearly frustrated, she threw her good hand in the air. "I keep lists of them on my computer and in a notebook stored in my safe-deposit box."

Wellborn checked the time on his phone. "It's too late for us to go to your bank today. We'll have to follow up tomorrow. In the meantime, I'd like a list of as many different passwords as you can remember."

She groaned. "I'll try."

"Your computer is still missing. If my tech people know your passwords, they can tap into the files from long distance."

"Good luck with that," she said. "My computer was a gift from Jamison before the divorce. He set up the encryption."

Clever move. Her ex-husband had been thinking ahead. He didn't expect investigators to look to his ex-wife for information, and if they did, he'd installed firewalls and the best cyberprotection money could buy. But SAC Wellborn wasn't about to give up. After he jotted down several passwords from Emily, he thanked her and headed out the door with his phone already pressed to his ear. The other law enforcement people followed him.

Connor glanced over at Beverly and asked, "Could you give us some privacy?"

"I'll wait outside."

When the door closed and they were alone, Emily slumped forward like a marionette whose strings had been cut. Her voice was ragged. "He played me for a fool."

"You're not the only one," he said. "Jamison betrayed a lot of people, many of those who invested money with him. He sure as hell conned me into thinking he was a good guy. That's not supposed to happen. I'm a lawyer. I should have known better."

"He used me."

Connor couldn't deny the painful truth. He sat on the bed beside her. When he touched her back, she cringed as though human contact was painful. But he didn't move away. Slowly, he massaged the knots of tension in her shoulders. "It's not your fault."

"I'm not so sure of that." She turned her head and looked up at him. Her blue eyes welled with unshed tears. "My mother would have told me that I deserved every bad thing that happened to me."

"Was she judgmental?"

"Worse, she was judgmental and drunk."

"And she was wrong." His hand slipped lower on her back to her jutting shoulder blades. Below that point, he felt the bandage supporting her injured ribs—a reminder of the hell she was going through. "You didn't do anything to deserve this."

"I thought I loved him, and I turned a blind eye to what Jamison was doing. I've heard that expression all my life and never really understood what it meant until now."

"Don't blame yourself, Emily."

"He purchased millions of dollars of artworks, and I helped him. I did the bidding at auctions and never worried about where the money was coming from."

A long time ago, Connor had questioned his former friend's good fortune. Sure, Jamison had come from a wealthy family and was doing well at his job, but he was spending almost as fast as he was earning and buying big-ticket items. There had been a trust fund, but Connor wouldn't have access to that until his thirty-fifth birthday, so the spending didn't make sense. Shortly after Connor had suggested they do an audit and set up a budget, Jamison shifted his business to another attorney. That should have raised a red flag.

"My vision wasn't twenty-twenty," Connor said. "I never expected him to do anything wrong or illegal."

"Illegal?" Alarmed, she sat up straight. "Did Jamison steal from people? Did he cause them to lose their life savings?"

It seemed really likely to Connor. The reason for a mysterious offshore account was to hide money— ill-gotten gains. "We won't know for sure until after Wellborn is done with his investigation."

With a surge of energy, she struggled to her feet and balanced on her good leg. "I have to get busy."

He maneuvered quickly to support her and make sure she didn't put weight on her sprained ankle. "First, you need to get better."

"Help me, Connor." Her right hand clung to his arm.

Her gaze implored him. "As soon as the paperwork is in order, I want you to sell that house in Aspen. The proceeds can be used to set up a fund for the relief of Jamison's victims. I need to fix this mess."

Her heart was in the right place, but it wasn't going to be easy to determine who was a victim and who was complicit. "I'll take care of the sale. What about the art?"

"For now, it can be on loan to schools and art museums. Later, I might sell that, too."

He encircled her in his arms and pulled her into an embrace. In spite of her energetic plans, her slender body felt as fragile as a baby bird. She rested her head on his shoulder and went silent. Her injuries had damaged her physically, but the wound of her latest betrayal at the hands of her ex-husband caused a far deeper pain.

"We'll take care of this," he said. "You can trust me."

"Can I?"

"I would never knowingly harm you, Emily."

She looked up at him, and he tightened his hold around her waist to keep her from falling. "Connor, I'm scared."

"Understandable. Somebody is trying to kill you."

"That's nothing compared to the hurt I'm feeling inside. How could I have been so wrong about Jamison? Why didn't I see him for what he really was?" Her lower lip trembled. "How can I ever open my heart again?"

There was no straightforward answer to that question. All he could do was hold her close and hope the hurt would go away and she would look around and see him standing beside her, ready and willing to give her all his love. He couldn't promise that their relationship would be perfect or that they'd never argue. But when he did make a promise, he wouldn't betray her. She could trust him with her battered heart.

Gently, he kissed her forehead beside the bandage covering her head wound. Her skin was hot, not feverish but heated. Lower, he kissed the tip of her nose. And then he slowly tasted her lips.

Passion raced through his veins, but he held back. Right now, she didn't need a lover. She needed a friend. And he was a patient man.

BACK IN HER hospital room, Emily kept her eyes closed, even though she wasn't sleeping. She was humiliated by the way she'd been conned and deeply regretful of the trouble she might have inadvertently caused her ex-husband's investors. When nurses and technicians came in and out of her room, she responded to their physical instructions. But that was the extent of her interaction. The only person who noticed her silence was Connor.

Beverly never did much talking. And Agent Wellborn had disappeared into his investigation. Only Connor stayed at her side. Steady and supportive, he held her hand and brought her things before she knew she wanted them. He encouraged her to eat her dinner even though she wasn't hungry because she needed to recover, to get her strength back.

In the physical therapy gym, she concentrated on her workout, using equipment that wouldn't put weight on her sprained ankle. Later that night, the lights were finally turned out, and it was as quiet as it ever got in a hospital. She asked for a sleeping pill and sank into a heavy slumber.

The next morning, her depression lessened when she gazed through the window at a pink-and-purple Rocky Mountain sunrise. She told herself that a new day meant new hope. As soon as she'd adjusted her bed to a sitting position, Connor gave her a little peck on the cheek. He'd already been awake for a while, long enough to wash up, if not to shave.

"You smell good," she said.

"Soap and water."

Part of her wanted to close her eyes and never confront the mess her life had become. The more practical side knew that action was required. "This is hard to deal with."

"You've had a whole series of life-changing shocks." He ticked them off on his fingers. "You got the inheritance, learned of the betrayal by Jamison and survived three murder attempts, which reminds me…there's something I wanted to ask about the operation you had in Aspen. The doctors—not Thorson but other docs— told us that you flatlined twice. Do you remember anything about it?"

"Like did I see white light and angels?"

"Or something else."

She'd always enjoyed the vision of the afterlife that included a welcoming party standing at the pearly gates. How could that possibly work? When her parents were alive, they hadn't really got along. In death, would old hostilities be forgotten? Emily couldn't imagine her distant father and her hostile mom with her endless resentment toward a daughter who demanded too much attention. Even their good times were tinged with ugliness. If she hadn't been able to escape into art, she didn't know how she would have survived.

And if her near-death experience didn't include her parents, who would be there? Surely not Jamison. She shuddered. "I don't think I want to remember."

"How come?"

"Let's just say that most of my guardian angels are carrying pitchforks." And she didn't want to be welcomed into their company. "We need to start making plans. There's a lot to do today. The number one, most important thing—I might get released."

"Dr. Troutman said it's a good possibility."

"I like Fish."

"And everything at the house should be ready for you," he said. "The security system complete with new door will be done by lunchtime, which is also when the housecleaning crew will finish up. Also, I've arranged for a part-time nurse and a physical therapist to come to the house twice a day to help with workouts."

"Damn, you're good. How would you like a permanent job as my assistant?"

"Sure, if you're willing to pay my rate for billable hours."

"Probably not." She was so accustomed to seeing him as a friend that she forgot he was really a highly paid New York attorney. "I really want to go to my gallery today. Maybe this afternoon."

"We can make that happen." He went toward the door. "I'm going for your tea and my coffee. When

I come back, we can talk about the rest of your day. Wellborn needs to schedule a time to get into your safe-deposit box."

While he was gone, Emily summoned the nurse's aide to help her into the bathroom, where she did the basics of brushing her teeth and splashing water on her face. Hesitantly, she looked into the mirror and was happy to see that the bruises were fading. The worst of the swelling had gone down. With makeup, she might pass for human.

Back in the bed, she pulled up the covers. "I should warn you, Beverly, about my Beretta. I'm not a very good shot."

"Are you planning to carry your weapon?" she asked.

"Not really." Her left arm was still in a cast, and the physical therapist hinted that she'd be using a cane with her right. Or she might be stuck in a wheelchair for another day or so. "I don't even know how I'd carry it."

"That's what I figured," the bodyguard said. "There's only one safety lesson you really need to learn."

"What's that?"

"Don't get shot." She stepped up to the bedside, unbuttoned the collared white shirt she wore under her suit jacket and pulled it open to show her undergarment. "This is a lightweight, breathable, bulletproof vest."

"It looks like a T-shirt."

"I hardly notice I have it on."

The door opened, and Emily craned her neck, expecting to see Connor. Instead, Phillip Riggs and his sister, Patricia, sauntered into her room.

Beverly reacted swiftly, pivoting and blocking access to the bed. Her tone was authoritative. "I have to ask you to leave."

Patricia stood her ground. She looked the bodyguard up and down. "You're a big one, aren't you?"

"Big enough to handle you," Beverly said as she took a step toward them. "Wait in the hall until Connor returns and gives the okay."

"Fine." Patricia sneered as she looked around the bodyguard. "I have a bone to pick with little missy here. It's not enough that she caused so much trouble for poor Phillip. Now she's destroyed my personal life."

"Hold it," Emily said. "What are you talking about?"

"Because of you, my fiancé, Dr. Eric Thorson, was forced to take a leave of absence. All he was trying to do was help you. And now he might lose his position at the hospital."

As far as Emily was concerned, Thorson deserved a much worse punishment. "You really can't blame me for what happened. I was in a coma."

"He's gone," she said. "He's not at his apartment and isn't answering his phone. And it's your fault."

You'll thank me later.

Emily pressed her lips together to keep from blurting out her opinion. Some things were better left unsaid.

Chapter Twelve

Connor exited the elevator carrying a tray with three beverages from the custom coffee shop in the lobby: a tea for Emily, black coffee for him and a latte for Beverly. As he walked, he mentally ran through the day's agenda and added a visit to her gallery to the list of things that needed to be done. He rounded the corner and saw Patricia and Phillip pacing the hallway outside Emily's room.

In a low, rasping voice, Connor demanded, "What the hell are you doing here?"

"No need to be rude." Patricia was cold and obnoxious. "May we have a word?"

"In a minute."

Beverly opened the door for him, and he entered Emily's room. As he handed out the beverages, he asked, "Did they tell you what they want?"

"I'm not sure," Emily said. "I think it's something about Thorson."

He raised his hot, aromatic coffee to his mouth and took a sip. "You don't have to talk to the Riggs family if you don't want to. They have no hold on you."

"I feel like I owe them an apology." She struggled with the cardboard cup, balancing it on her lap and flipping open the hole in the lid with her right hand. "I thought they were the ones trying to kill me, but now I'm almost certain that Kate is behind the assaults."

"Don't be so sure."

Being a lawyer had taught him to expect the unexpected. Kate looked like the number one suspect, but her motives didn't add up. When she first talked to Emily, she wanted information. The search at the house had been about finding the bank account number and the password. He couldn't see what Kate had to gain by having Emily dead.

There was a sharp rap at the door. "Let us in," Patricia said harshly.

"It's okay," Emily said with a sigh. "We might as well get this over with."

When Beverly opened the door, Patricia and Phillip spilled inside. Connor took a closer look at them. The unflappable Patricia wasn't put together perfectly. Her straight brown hair was askew. A wig? He never knew she wore a wig. Her clothes looked like she'd slept in them. And her makeup had smeared into raccoon eyes. Any sympathy he might have felt for her vanished when she opened her mouth.

"I demand to know," Patricia said. "Where is my fiancé?"

"The police are looking for him," Connor said.

"Whatever for? He's done nothing wrong."

"He's a witness. That means he's involved."

She tugged on her hair. "This is all a terrible misunderstanding. When he moved Emily into the ambulance, he was only trying to help me."

"To what end?" Connor asked. "Kidnapping?"

"Never." She stiffened her spine. Beside her, Phillip mimicked her posture. Clearly, he was the follower in this family dynamic.

"Be honest," Emily said from the bed. "We've never been close. Why did you want to take me to your home?"

"My primary concern was, of course, your well-being," Patricia said. "And I will admit that because you had just inherited a valuable piece of our family property, I wanted to make sure you did the right thing."

"By *the right thing*," Connor said, "you mean giving the house back to the family."

Phillip piped up, "It's a great house. I've lived there for years."

"You have," Emily said. "Exactly how long?"

"At least six years," he said. "I took care of the place when you and Jamison weren't there. When you came to town, I moved in with Aunt Glenda so you'd have your privacy. I love that house. I don't want to leave. Jamison knew that."

"I'm sorry," Emily said.

An expression of concern crossed her face, and Connor was amazed by the depth of her compassion. The Riggs family—every last one of them—had been bitchy toward her from the moment she first said hello. He couldn't believe she'd cut them any slack.

"I've got a solution," he said to Phillip. "Emily is going to sell the house. If you want it so much, you can buy it."

Patricia laughed out loud. "Phillip doesn't have that kind of money."

Other people in the family, including Patricia, could finance the purchase for her hapless younger brother, but Connor didn't want to squabble. "In a few weeks, it'll be on the market."

"What about the art?" Phillip asked.

Emily brightened, as she always did when discussing the subject that was nearest and dearest to her heart. "I'm planning to loan most of it to museums. Are there any pieces you especially like? The Degas? The Banksy lithographs?"

After a moment of hemming and hawing, he said, "I like the cowboy picture."

"The Remington," she said. "Good choice. Maybe we can figure out some way that you can keep it."

"Yes, yes, lovely," Patricia drawled. "Let's get back to what's really important—my missing fiancé. What do you intend to do about him?"

He sensed a symphony of false notes in this romance. Patricia had never been a warm person, and Thorson was a narcissistic jerk. "How did you two meet?"

She wrapped her black knee-length cape more tightly around her and shrugged her bony shoulders. "I don't really remember. It was one of those hospital fund-raisers."

"So he didn't sweep you off your feet," Connor said drily.

"We're adults." She spread her cape like a vampire bat. "Our relationship is built on mutual goals and desires. Eric appreciates my financial abilities. And I respect his talent. He's more than an ER doctor, you know. He has a world-class reputation as a virologist."

"Has he cured anything I might have heard of?"

"He's been an integral part of teams in Central Asia and Africa. After we're married next year, I plan to set up a research center for him."

"Next year?" Emily questioned.

"It would have been sooner, but I decided to wait for a decent interval after Jamison's death."

"To see how you fared in your cousin's will," Connor said.

"A sensible plan."

Not exactly a starry-eyed declaration of love, but these two were, in their own way, made for each other. Patricia got to call herself a doctor's wife and parade around her Norse demigod husband while Thorson received funding for his virus research.

"If we hear anything about him, we'll let you know," he said. "Let me ask you a question. How well do you know Kate Sylvester?"

"She's an acquaintance."

Not according to the scant information he had. "She was staying with Phillip."

"Hey," he said, "I've got a girlfriend. But Kate is an excellent snowboarder. When she comes to town, I let her use one of the bedrooms and—"

"That's enough," Patricia said. She looked down her nose, an expression that failed to intimidate, given her smeared makeup. "Why are you interested in Kate?"

Not wanting to show his hand, he brushed her question aside. "I wondered why Jamison left her a Rolex in his will."

"Don't ask me. I don't understand half the things Jamison did."

When the breakfast tray from the hospital kitchen was delivered, Connor chased Patricia and Phillip from the room. He settled into the chair beside Emily's bed and watched with approval as she dug into the scrambled eggs and bacon. She looked healthier today. In spite of yesterday's painful revelations, she continued to recover.

The visit from Patricia and Phillip caused him to reconsider some of their conclusions about Kate. "Did they seem suspicious to you?"

"With the Riggs family," she said, "there's usually an ulterior motive. I'm pretty sure that they weren't whisking me away from the hospital because they were concerned."

"Patricia admitted that they wanted to keep an eye on you."

"Why? At that point, nobody knew how bad my injuries were. I could have been in a coma for months."

Keeping Emily under their thumb would have worked well for the Riggs family. They could have maintained her coma, supposedly for her own good, while they manipulated the property away from her. "We need evidence," he said.

She nibbled on a piece of bacon. "You could talk to Adam, the ambulance guy."

As soon as she said the name, he pulled his cell phone from his pocket and put through a call to Adam.

When she had started waking up prematurely, he and Adam had supposed it was due to a changed dosage in the sedative that she'd been given. Connor had seen the switched IV bag as a threat, designed to bring her around to consciousness too soon.

Adam answered quickly. "Hey, Connor, how's our girl?"

"She'll probably get out of the hospital today or to-morrow," he said. "Thanks again for everything you did."

"Anytime you need somebody for a free helo ride to Denver, give me a call."

"Did you ever get the switched IV bag tested?"

"I brought it back to the Aspen hospital," Adam said. "The lab people told me the dosage wasn't what had been prescribed."

"What about fingerprints?"

"I gave the bag to Sandoval. Check with him." Static noise interrupted their call. "I've got to roll, Connor. Good to hear from you."

He disconnected the call. The assumptions he and Adam had made were correct. Somebody had tried to tamper with her treatment. As far as he could tell, Kate hadn't been involved while they were in Aspen. It wasn't until they had got to Denver that he spotted her at the hospital wearing scrubs. Wellborn and the DPD had been looking for her, but she'd disappeared.

His suspicions shifted back toward the Riggs family and Patricia's doctor fiancé. Thorson would have un-derstood how the IV was used and the danger it might be to Emily.

"This is going to sound crazy," he said, "but I find myself agreeing with Patricia."

Her blue eyes opened wide. "About what?"

"We need to find Thorson."

The doctor had some explaining to do.

INSTEAD OF TROOPING along with Wellborn to the bank, Emily opted for medical care. Fish and his team did a few more tests and were pleased with her progress. Her seizure continued to puzzle them, and the blood tests failed to identify any foreign substance that might have caused that reaction. There was no evidence, but she'd suffered a seizure after Connor had seen Kate Sylvester in scrubs at the hospital. Could Kate have somehow infected her with an untraceable toxin? Though she didn't want to take the next logical step, Emily couldn't help wondering if a similar poison had been used to cause Jamison's fatal illness.

His mysterious death loomed at the center of everything and caused the threats to her life. Kate would go to great lengths to get the account number and the password that she thought Emily knew. The Riggs family was trying to thwart Jamison's will and reclaim her inheritance.

She was angry at him for putting her into this situation. But how could she rail at a dead man? He didn't deserve to die so young.

She perked up when Dr. Parris removed the cast on her arm and replaced it with a much smaller version that covered the back of her hand and stopped below her elbow. Moving her arm to different positions was sheer pleasure.

"How long will I have this cast?" she asked.

"Less than a month," Parris said. "Now, let's take a look at that ankle."

As she removed the plastic boot, she issued a series of instructions. "You need to keep icing it, elevate it when possible and use compression."

Emily looked down at her sprain. Bruised and swollen, her ankle was not a pretty sight. "Can I walk on it?"

"If you use the boot, you can put weight on it as long as it doesn't hurt. But I don't trust you with that solution. You're a woman who pushes herself. You might over-estimate your mobility and worsen the injury."

"Yeah, I do that. Trying to run when I shouldn't even be walking."

"Let's keep you in a wheelchair for as long as possible. You need to recover slowly. We can start with a splint and a cane."

"Cool." She glanced toward the backup bodyguard, a square-shouldered guy with a beard, who was standing in for Beverly. She asked him, "What do you think, Schultz? Can you get me a cane with a sword inside?"

"I'm pretty sure Beverly wouldn't go for that."

"We don't have to tell her," Emily said.

"No swords," Dr. Parris said. "Don't strain the sprain. Get it?"

"Got it."

In the physical therapy gym, she learned how to use a cane and practiced walking the perimeter of the area. When her leg was tired, she dropped into a wheelchair and allowed the therapist to whisk her back to her room, where she took her time with a long shower and had a change of clothes. Only a few garments required help from a nurse's aide. On top, she wore a short-sleeved T-shirt under the lavender velour sweatshirt with the cut sleeve. Her new cast was smaller but still too bulky to fit neatly inside a sleeve. Her slacks were khakis. She had a purple sock on the injured ankle and a purple sneaker on her good foot.

Back in her room, she was seated in the comfortable recliner, with her ankle elevated on the footrest. She waved Schultz toward her. "Do you like to draw?"

"I'm no artist." Behind his trim brown beard, the corners of his mouth turned down. "My three-year-old daughter makes prettier pictures than I do."

"No problem," she said. "I have a set of markers in my purse. Grab one and sign your name on my cast."

After gathering a few more scribbles and signatures from hospital staff, she was beginning to feel restless. This was more than enough time in the hospital. She wanted to go to her gallery and was anxious to show Connor the work she'd done, transforming a simple storefront into a warm, inviting space. As soon as possible, she needed to meet with her part-time staff. There was work to be done before the scheduled showing of Southwestern art. She needed to curate, to plan and to finalize her contract with the mariachis.

Connor strode into the room accompanied by Beverly. When he saw Emily, he stopped in his tracks. "Well, look at you," he said. "A smaller cast on your arm and no plastic boot."

His complimentary tone matched her upbeat energy.

She pointed to her forehead. "And Fish took off the big bandage."

"With your hair combed over, I can't even tell you were whacked." He placed the box he'd been carrying on one of the small tables with wheels that he whipped across the floor and parked beside her. "You're almost back to normal. Not that you've ever been normal or average. You're way above. Top-notch."

She pointed to the box. "A present?"

"I should have brought you something beautiful. Hang on a minute. I can run down to the lobby and get more flowers."

His enthusiasm warmed her inside. This man—this very handsome man—thought she deserved bouquets and beauty. If he got this excited about clean hair and a velour sweatshirt, she wondered what would happen if she dared to put on a filmy, lacy negligee. The thought made her blush, and she pushed the image to the back of her mind to be savored later. "What's in the box?"

"The contents of your safe-deposit box. I did like you said, piled it all in here without looking at anything."

"Does Wellborn need to be here before I open it?"

"I promised to contact him if you find a password." He scooted a chair across the room and sat beside her. "His tech people got access to your files that were saved onto the cloud but haven't uncovered anything significant."

"If Jamison didn't want it to be found, he knew how to keep stuff secret."

She lifted the lid and peeked inside. Mostly, her safe-deposit box had contained documents. There were a couple of small velvet jewelry boxes for special pieces, letter-sized envelopes with mementos tucked inside, a diary from her teen years and a five-by-seven notebook with a hot-pink cover. She plucked out the notebook and started flipping through pages, looking for the right password.

"What happens," she asked, "if I can't find it?"

"I asked Wellborn about that. Worst-case scenario, he'll take you to the Caymans, where you can find the bank and use your fingerprints to get whatever is in there."

"Another trip to the island doesn't sound too terrible." She wiggled the fingers on her right hand at him. "All I have to do is leave my prints."

"There is a downside."

"Of course." She braced for the inevitable downer.

"If Wellborn is able to get into the offshore account and Kate isn't, she'll need to prevent his access. She'll want to stop you from helping the feds. It's another motive."

"That's just what I need—another reason for somebody to want me dead." It seemed like every time they uncovered a potential clue, they found nothing but a dead end. She went back to the beginning. "Have you heard anything about the truck?"

"The last thing I heard from Sandoval was that he hadn't found the truck or your laptop. Are you sure you had it with you?"

"I remember thinking I should take it in case I was too tired to drive home and had to spend the night in the mountains. I figured I could catch up on emails."

She frowned at the numbers scribbled in her pink notebook. "I can't swear that I actually put the computer in the car."

"You're calm about it," he said. "If I get separated from my laptop or my phone or any of my electronic devices, I go a little crazy."

She liked to think that long ago, when she'd jotted everything in notebooks, was a simpler time, but that just wasn't true. Her electronics made it easy to keep track of virtually everything. She pointed to a page in the pink notebook. "This is the number for a savings account. Not the one in the Caymans, but I might have used a similar password."

"What is it?"

"Warhol," she said, "because Andy Warhol did that painting of a one-dollar bill."

He tapped the keys on his phone and made a note. "Anything else?"

Her little notebook was filled with page after page of notations. Some were important, like the account number, while others were reminders or recipes or phone numbers. "It's hard to believe I scribbled all these details. Now I keep everything on my phone and my computer."

"It's safer that way. Your information is stored with a long-distance server, right?"

"Supposedly." Though she seldom had reason to contact the cloud, where her files were stored, she trusted that the system was effective as long as she kept the account paid and current. She closed the notebook and looked up at him. "I'll set this aside for later. Right now, I'm ready to go to my gallery."

"And I'm ready to see it."

He leaned over and gave her a friendly kiss on the cheek that both pleased and annoyed. She liked their familiarity but didn't want to continue on the platonic path. As a bosom buddy, he ought to pay more attention to her breasts. She wanted their sizzling chemistry to ignite into a full, luscious blaze.

Mobilizing to leave the hospital was a complicated operation, and Beverly took charge, ordering Schultz to bring the van around to the front exit and arranging with the hospital staff to keep the stuff from her safe-deposit box in a secure location.

Less than a half hour later, Beverly turned to her and Connor with further instructions. "Schultz will drive. Connor and I will ride in back. Emily is in the passenger seat. I've arranged for O'Brien to meet us at the gallery. He has information from the DPD and from his trip to Aspen."

"Evidence?" she asked hopefully.

"I don't know," Beverly said. "Solving the crime isn't my job."

"Maybe give it a try," Emily suggested. "I'll bet you'd make an outstanding detective."

"I would. But it doesn't interest me."

Connor pushed her wheelchair through the corridors, into the elevator and down to the first floor. When they went through the double doors at the front of the building, she turned her face toward the bright sunshine and reveled in the caress of a September breeze. In a landscaped area near the parking garage, the leaves on five slender aspen trees had turned to gold. She'd only been out of commission a few days, but it felt like a lot longer.

Instead of the ambulance cab, they were able to use a regular van. At the passenger door, Connor helped her inside. He took her wheelchair, folded it up and stowed it in the rear of the van. Beverly made sure she was safely inside before she closed the door.

Emily put on her safety belt, glanced toward the street and froze. Fear smacked her right between the eyes. She blinked wildly but still saw it. A black truck turned right at the corner.

Chapter Thirteen

Emily held her breath and stared straight ahead through the windshield. She wanted to scream but held back. She couldn't allow herself to burst into hysterics every time she saw a black truck. This was Colorado, where lots of people drove trucks, even in the city.

She heard Connor's voice. He sounded hollow as though calling to her from the bottom of a well instead of the back seat of the van, and he seemed to be asking if she was all right.

"Fine," she said quickly. "I'm fine."

"You look startled," he said.

Had he always been so talented at reading her mind? Though she was hoping the two of them would get close, she didn't like being so very transparent. Glass was fragile, easy to break. And she needed to be strong.

Determined to hold it together, she changed the subject. "You're going to like my gallery."

Trying not to sound like a tour guide or a real estate agent, she described the five-block area in an older part of town near Etta Morton Elementary. Most of the run-down businesses had been renovated into art galleries, craft stores, cafés, tapas bars, yoga studios and more. Every first Friday of the month, the Morton Merchants' Association sponsored an open house. On holidays, they threw street fairs. "I checked out a lot of neighborhoods all over town and worked at other galleries before I found the perfect space."

"And you call it Calico Cat," he said, "but not the imaginary calico named Taffy."

"Not imaginary."

"Why that name?"

While the van crept through afternoon traffic, she watched the vehicles around them and behind them, looking for the black truck. Though she told herself there was no way he'd ambush them on the road in front of all these witnesses, she couldn't erase her fear.

"Calico Cat," she said. "I never had pets when I was a kid. My mom hated the mess. But I found a mangy stuffed animal—a calico cat. I whispered my secrets to the calico and told her my dreams, but that's not why I chose the name. The Japanese think a calico cat is good luck."

"Excellent reason."

When they turned off Downing Street, the traffic lessened. Since it was too early for the dinner crowd, the Morton neighborhood wasn't too hectic. Her shop was around the corner from a clothing store that specialized in woven organic-hemp purses and loose-fitting shirts. The sign hanging over the door of her gallery was shaped like the namesake cat. Decorative ironwork covered the front window and the door.

From the back seat, Beverly issued an order to

Schultz. "Drive down the alley to the back. I want to check out the security."

"It's solid," Emily said. "Before I moved in, this storefront was a pot dispensary. Those guys really know how to guard their product."

After Beverly gave the okay on the back door, they circled around the block and returned to the street in front of the store. Schultz found a parking space on the other side of the alley, less than fifty steps from the door.

"Give me your keys," Beverly said. "I'll unlock the door."

"You'll also need the code to deactivate the alarm system." Emily rattled off the code numbers. "The box is to the left above the light switches."

"I'll find it. After I open up and take a look around inside to make sure it's safe, I'll signal to the boys. They'll get your wheelchair and bring you inside."

"I brought my cane," she said. "I could walk."

"We'll do this my way." Beverly was calm but authoritative. "I want you to stay in the wheelchair until we get inside. Then you can hop, skip or jump. Fair enough?"

The precautions seemed extreme, but Emily didn't argue. Her bossy bodyguard was an expert. If the black truck showed up again, she wanted to be with somebody who took control and kicked butt. And so, they sat in the van and waited for Beverly's signal.

As soon as she waved, Schultz and Connor went into action. Their moves were efficient, almost choreographed. Connor brought the wheelchair to the passenger side and opened the door so she could climb out and get seated.

Schultz walked next to her on the street side.

Beverly had taken a position in front of the gallery. Like Schultz, her hand rested on the butt of her holstered weapon.

Emily heard the *pop-pop-pop* of muffled gunshots.

A heavy impact slammed into her upper chest. She jolted backward in the chair.

Everything went black.

CONNOR THREW HIMSELF in front of her. Too late, he was too late. Emily was unconscious. She'd been hit.

He wouldn't give up. Not now. Not ever. *Move fast. Get her to safety!* He scrambled to drag her limp body from the wheelchair. Throwing her over his shoulder wasn't an option. Not with her bruised ribs. He held her under the arms and knees.

Schultz stood in front of them both. He scanned the area. His gun was drawn.

"Over here," Beverly yelled as she held the shop door wide open. "Connor, bring Emily inside. Schultz, go after the shooter."

Connor staggered through the door, taking care not to bump her head or any other part of her body. He avoided looking down at the woman in his arms. If she was bleeding, he didn't want to see it. He couldn't bear to watch her die.

Inside the gallery, Beverly turned off the overhead lights and rushed him toward an antique door near the back of the gallery. She twisted the brass knob and yanked it open. "Stay in this storage room. Keep the door closed."

"Wait," he said. "I should call 9-1-1."

"No," a small voice objected.

He was stunned. "What?"

Emily wiggled in his arms. "Don't call 9-1-1."

"You're not dead."

"Not yet."

Beverly turned on the lights in the storage room, and he looked down into Emily's clear, wide-open eyes. There were no discernible smears of blood on her body. He didn't know how or why, but she appeared to be all right.

"Put me down," she said, "and go after that son of a bitch."

"That's my job," Beverly said. "Connor, stay in this room, and keep an eye on her."

"Why here?"

"No windows," she said.

Beverly dashed from the room and closed the door behind her. Connor couldn't think of what he was supposed to do next. His usually organized mind was overwhelmed by a tsunami of adrenaline. His pulse was racing. Too much had happened in a very short time span. He was off balance, unable to get his bearings.

"Connor, are you all right?"

"I should be asking you that question."

She'd been attacked…again. And he had failed to protect her…again.

He had to get it together, starting now. He set Emily down on a folding chair near the door, hunkered down beside Emily and patted her knee, reassuring her and himself at the same time.

"I don't understand what happened. I heard the shots. You slumped forward." Trying to calm himself, he exhaled slowly. "I thought you were hit."

"I was."

"You're telling me that you were shot."

"Correct, but I'm pretty much okay."

For sure, he was glad. But he had to admit that her ability to survive against all odds was beginning to get spooky. "I'm going to need more information."

She unzipped her sweatshirt and pulled the boatneck of her light blue T-shirt down to reveal an undergarment. "Bulletproof vest," she said. "Beverly said I had to wear one whenever I went outside."

"Where were you hit?"

"Here." She winced as she rubbed at her upper chest below her left shoulder. "It feels like I got punched really hard."

"Let me take a look."

When he eased her casted left arm out of the sweatshirt, she winced. From the little he knew, a bulletproof vest wasn't like a suit of armor. The bullet didn't pierce the skin, but the impact was still felt. He reached inside her T-shirt and unfastened the strap for the vest, which he carefully pulled away from her shoulder. A reddish-purple bruise marred her smooth pale skin.

She twisted her neck, trying to see the area. "How bad is it?"

"Bad enough that you need to get it checked out by a doctor."

"I'll do that," she said. "I didn't want to call 9-1-1 right now because I wanted Beverly and Schultz to focus on going after the person who shot me. Did you see him? Maybe it wasn't a man. Was it Kate?"

"I don't know." He replaced the strap on the vest. As long as she was out in public, she needed all the protection she could get. "I saw a couple of people milling around at the street corner outside the hemp shop. If one of them had been pointing a gun, I sure as hell would have noticed. Maybe he was in a car."

"Or a truck," she said.

For the first time, he looked around the storage room and saw a giant papier-mâché skull decorated with bright flowers. Four skeletons, wearing sombreros and serapes with orange, yellow and green stripes, danced across the back wall, where a decorated coffin leaned ominously. "What's going on in here?"

"Dia de los Muertos," she said. "The Day of the Dead is next month, and I'm storing some of the artwork. My gallery is sponsoring a float for the parade on the weekend before. It's not a holiday I usually get excited about, but I keep thinking about how Jamison died so young."

"You miss him."

"Oh, no," she said, "that's not how I feel about my ex-husband, especially not after the past couple of days. They say that on *Dia de los Muertos*, the veil between life and death is lifted, and you can communicate with the dead. I'd like the chance to tell him how I hate being used and manipulated."

"Or you could ask him for the password."

She gave a short laugh. "I don't like being angry like this. I'd rather stick to the Day of the Dead tradition of dancing with death to celebrate life."

"I have another idea for celebrating. It doesn't involve skeletons or skulls or floats or parades." His gaze mingled with hers. He was fascinated by the many facets of her sapphire eyes. "I'd like to throw a private party for just you and me. Maybe we could have a bottle of wine, listen to some music."

Her slight, subtle grin told him that she was on the same wavelength and had also been thinking about time they could spend together. Soon, they'd have their chance.

The door at the front of the store crashed open, and he jumped to his feet, ready to defend her.

Beverly called out, "It's me and Schultz. O'Brien is with us, too."

Emily stood and grasped his arm for support. "I want to hear what they found out."

"Are you supposed to be walking around?"

"It's okay as long as I don't strain the sprain. You can help by putting your arm around my waist and matching your steps to mine. I want to go to my office at the back of the shop. Beverly will approve of that space. There's only one small window."

He followed her instructions. Wrapping his arm around her gave him pleasure. At six foot three, he was at least eight inches taller, but they fitted together nicely. Her body rubbed against him as they shuffled slowly across the slate-tiled floor.

Beverly had turned on the overhead lights, and he had a chance to view some of the pieces on display. Her shop was three times as long as it was wide, and Emily had added several partitions to add more hanging space. The art ranged from photography to watercolor to oil, and many different styles were represented. Though the walls were mostly white, she'd used wood and plastic trim to give texture and contrast.

"You did a great job in here," he said.

"Thank you."

She sank into the swivel chair behind an L-shaped desk with a sleek black acrylic top. Her office at the farthest end of the shop was open to the rest of the gallery but set apart with strategically placed partitions to give privacy. A break room with a kitchen counter, microwave and sink was on the opposite wall.

She waved toward the fridge. "Help yourselves. There's wine, beer and soft drinks."

Connor greeted O'Brien. He hadn't spoken to the detective in person since they discovered Emily's ransacked house together. "Beverly said you have information."

"Not enough," he muttered. "I'll fill you in."

"Something to drink?"

"I wouldn't mind a beer."

Since Emily was laid up, Connor played host, serving craft beers to O'Brien and Schultz. Beverly got herself a glass of tap water. And Emily wanted an orange soda. He took the same and then sat at a round table with four chairs. O'Brien joined him. Schultz sprawled on the long Scandinavian-style sofa while Beverly remained standing, ready to leap into action at any given moment.

"Tell me about the Denver PD," Connor said. "The CSI team was all over Emily's house. Did they find anything?"

"No witnesses. They interviewed neighbors and other people who might be in the area." O'Brien raked his fingers through his graying hair. "There were fingerprints. When they ran them through the system, nothing popped."

"What does that mean?" Emily asked.

"Nothing showed up in criminal databases for Colorado or for the FBI. Others fingerprints could be logically explained, like your neighbor and a woman who works for a professional cleaning service."

She asked, "How soon will my house be ready for me to move back in?"

"I just came from there," he said. "It's been cleaned, security added and the door repaired. It's ready now."

That had to make her happy. Connor knew she was itching to get home, which seemed strange, given everything that had happened to her—including someone breaking into her house and going through her things. Maybe she found strength in her own space and felt less vulnerable.

He turned to the detective. "You've been in Aspen. Find anything useful?"

"It's so damned pretty." He took a long pull from his beer bottle and loosened his necktie. "That mountain scenery is why I moved to Colorado. Glenda Riggs is not a charming woman, but her ranch has got to be one of the most beautiful sights on earth. That's the kind of place where I want to retire. I'm getting close to that age. I know I don't look it, but I'm fifty-six."

"No kidding." Connor said with a teasing grin, "I would've guessed seventy-seven."

"Wise guy."

Actually, it would have been difficult to pinpoint O'Brien's age. He was in good physical condition, but the lines in his face showed a lifetime of experience. "While you were admiring the peaks, did you get a chance to talk to Deputy Sandoval?"

"I did. He and his crew are working over Emily's smashed-up Hyundai. They haven't located her laptop."

"Did he tell you about the switched IV bag?"

"Pitkin County Forensics found smudges on the bag that might indicate someone handled it with gloved hands. The only distinct prints belonged to you and the ambulance driver."

Emily exhaled a frustrated sigh. "So we struck out in Aspen and in Denver."

"It's not a total loss. I've got a long list of names to check out, including people who were at the reading of the will. I broke them into two groups. First, there are those loyal to the Riggs family. Second are Jamison's business associates, who would also know Kate Sylvester."

The investigation wasn't a blazing success, but Connor could see progress. Various directions were taking shape. "We should talk about what just happened here—the shooting."

"I caught a glimpse of the shooter," Schultz said.

"Somebody in a hooded sweatshirt stuck their arm out of the passenger side of a car and fired. I heard three shots. I think he was using a silencer."

"A good marksman," Beverly said under her breath. "Only three shots to get a direct hit."

"They drove off fast," Schultz said.

O'Brien asked, "Did you get a license plate?"

"The last two numbers were seven and three, Colorado plates. They were gone before I could read more."

While Beverly and O'Brien peppered Schultz with questions about whether the shooter used a silencer and the escape route of the vehicle, Connor took a moment to digest this significant bit of information. There was a driver and a shooter—two people. Either Kate Sylvester was working with a partner or Patricia and Phillip Riggs had jumped back to the top of the suspect list.

"Excuse me," Emily interrupted. "I have to know. What kind of vehicle was it?"

"A dark gray Chevy sedan," Schultz said. "Why?"

"I saw a black truck at the hospital."

Chapter Fourteen

Aware that she'd dropped a bombshell, Emily swiveled in her desk chair and glanced around the room, looking from one person to the next until she confronted Connor's hard gaze. She explained, "I couldn't tell if it was the same truck that ran me off the road. I didn't notice dents or damage. It pulled away after we'd all loaded into the van."

"They were watching," Beverly said. "That explains the coincidence of a shooter who appeared outside your shop as soon as we arrived."

"But the shooter wasn't in a truck," Emily said.

"There's a second vehicle," Connor said in measured tones. "A shooter and a driver. There are at least two people involved."

Though he didn't yell and wave his arms, she knew he was mad at her. Her inclination was to apologize and avoid conflict. But why should she? She'd done nothing wrong. "I didn't point out the truck because I wasn't sure. I didn't want to set off a false alarm."

Instead of reassuring her, he turned toward O'Brien. "Can the truck and the sedan be tracked through traffic? In Manhattan, there are enough security cameras on stoplights and ATMs and buildings for the police to follow the camera feeds and do surveillance, especially when they know what kind of car they're looking for."

"I can arrange something, maybe not through law enforcement. I have my own channels." O'Brien took his phone from his pocket. "Still, before we do anything, we should make a report to the police."

"You'll find us at the hospital," Connor said as he stood. "Emily needs to be checked out by a doctor. Beverly, you'll come with us."

"I'm all right," Emily protested. The bruise where she'd been shot throbbed, but she could handle the pain. "I can stay and talk to the police."

"It's not necessary," he said as he strode the length of the gallery and grabbed her wheelchair, which one of the bodyguards had left at the front door. "Beverly, which is more secure, the front door or the back?"

"Back," she said. "I'll pull the van around."

He whipped the wheelchair up beside her, put on the brake and took her arm to help her move from her swivel chair.

She jerked her arm from his grasp. "I don't need help."

"Suit yourself."

Balancing on her good leg and putting very little weight on the sprained ankle, she maneuvered her way into the chair. A full-scale eruption was building inside her, and she sealed her lips so she wouldn't snap at him or Beverly as they shuffled her around like a sack of potatoes. In moments, they were in the van with Connor behind the steering wheel.

So what if he was angry? That didn't give him the right to order her around and refuse to listen to her. After she'd been married awhile, Jamison had started treating her the same way, like a child who was incapable of making her own decisions. When she'd objected to her ex-husband's controlling attitude, he had placated her with gifts and had told her that he enjoyed taking care of her. Sometimes she liked being pampered, but there were occasions when she chafed under his condescending pats on the head. She hoped Connor wouldn't turn out to be more of the same.

Sure, he respected her as a friend. But what if their relationship turned into something more? He already felt obliged to protect her. Too easily, protection could become control. She didn't want him to watch over her every move, to dictate her life.

She wasn't helpless—far from it. Emily had pretty much raised herself after her parents' death. She'd escaped her annoying uncle and put herself through school on scholarships. At age twenty-two, she'd found a job in the highly competitive art market of New York. To top it off, she'd married a rich man. Her life should have been a success. Why did she feel like such a disaster?

In the driver's seat beside her, Connor was silent.

An apology was out of the question, but she hated feeling so distant from him. "Is there something you want to say to me?"

"I'm not buying your false-alarm excuse."

"I don't care if you do."

He stared through the windshield at the bumper-to-bumper traffic. Though it wasn't even four o'clock, rush hour had already begun. "I don't get it. Why didn't you say something? You know we're all searching for the black truck. Did you think we wouldn't believe you?"

"Maybe."

His jaw clenched. "You've got to trust us, Emily. Trust me. I'm on your side. You don't have to handle this alone."

"I was scared." The words jumped out before she could stop them. Even worse, she felt tears flooding her eyes. She didn't want to be a crybaby. Her mom had taught her better; she sneered at those who wept.

At a stoplight, he turned his head and studied her. His dark eyes softened. He reached across the center console and rested his hand on her arm above the cast. "I'm sorry."

His sensitivity melted the hard core inside her. Her guard dropped. Was there anything more macho than a man who could admit when he'd made a mistake? She swabbed away her tears before they slipped down her cheeks.

"You were right about one thing," she said. "I'm glad we're going back to the hospital. Even with the vest, I'm feeling the pain."

From the back seat, Beverly said, "The bruise will go away in a couple of days. You're lucky you weren't hit in your cracked ribs."

Her ribs were feeling good in comparison to the new contusion. "Have you been shot before?"

"Half a dozen times," she said casually. "Only once

without the vest. I was in the hospital for two weeks, and that was when I decided to leave the marines."

"But you became a bodyguard. That's not exactly a nonviolent profession."

"A life without risk isn't worth living. Charles Lindbergh said that."

When they parked at the emergency entrance to the hospital, Beverly was hypervigilant as they traveled the short distance from the van to the door. Rather than going through the ER doctors, Connor put through a call to Troutman and Parris.

Dr. Parris arrived first. She dashed into the waiting area with her ponytail bouncing from side to side. "A gunshot? Really?"

"I like to keep you on your toes," Emily said. "It's starting to hurt."

"This way." She'd been involved with Emily's case long enough to know that Beverly would follow them wherever they went.

Before they swooshed through the first set of doors, Emily waved to Connor. "I'll meet you back at the room."

She wasn't angry at him anymore. And she hoped he felt the same.

CONNOR STAYED IN the waiting area outside the ER until Troutman arrived. After he greeted the doctor, he said, "I wasn't sure if I needed to call you to handle a gunshot wound."

"Was she shot in the head?"

"No."

"You don't need me." Troutman's expression turned thoughtful as he stroked the line of his narrow jaw. "But I'm glad you called. I'll walk with you back to her room."

They fell into step together as they went down the first-floor corridors leading to the elevators. At the gift shop, Connor paused, wondering if he should run inside and grab a bouquet of roses to underline his apology. "I probably owe her some flowers."

"You did something wrong," Troutman deduced. "White tulips mean *I'm sorry* in the language of flowers. I always give my wife a bouquet when I've forgotten an anniversary or messed something up."

"I wasn't wrong." He was right to demand that she trust him and tell him everything, but he should have realized how frightened she was. "It was a mistake."

"She'll forgive you," Troutman said as they boarded the elevator. "I see how you two look at each other."

"It's that obvious?"

"You bet," the doctor said as they boarded the elevator. "But that's not why I wanted to confer with you."

At her floor, Troutman said hello to several of the staff. It wasn't until they were in Emily's private room that he got to the point.

"I know you've been working with the FBI, which means Emily's case is more than a hit-and-run car accident. I'm concerned about the results from her blood tests. The lab found a small amount of a toxic substance that appears to be organic in nature. Before I turn this information over to our toxicology technicians, I wanted to know if I should consult with the FBI."

"Is this substance a poison?"

"That's the simple explanation. It appears to be quickly absorbed into the body, which makes it untraceable." He shrugged his shoulders and flashed his charming grin. "It's not my field. I'm not an expert."

But Connor knew someone who was. Patricia had bragged about her virologist boyfriend, Dr. Eric Thorson. "I'll put you in touch with Special Agent in Charge Wellborn."

"Is this something I should keep to myself?"

"That's probably best."

"The FBI." The doctor's grin got even wider. "Kind of exciting."

Connor could do without any extra drama, but this merry-go-round wouldn't stop until the bad guys were caught. "On a different subject, Emily wants to go home tomorrow."

"If you've arranged for a nurse, I don't see any reason why she shouldn't be released. My office will schedule a follow-up in about a week."

When the doctor left, Connor sat in the recliner chair that he'd come to think of as Emily's throne. He popped up the footrest, stretched out his legs and leaned his head back, enjoying this moment of quiet before he put in a call to Wellborn.

With every new piece of information, the trail of evidence got more twisted and complex. He tried to put Troutman's mystery toxin into perspective. Right before Emily's seizure, he'd seen Kate Sylvester. It was possible that Kate had infected her with the toxin, either with an injection or some airborne method. A similar exposure might have led to Jamison's death. But how would a Wall Street broker get her mitts on an organic poison—a substance so exotic that it had Troutman baffled?

An expert like Thorson, who had a background in virology would know about complex toxins. Connor had instinctively disliked that guy from the moment they'd met. He'd questioned Thorson's competence, but it was hard to think of an ER doctor as a murderer. Also, Thorson was Patricia's fiancé. Why would he help Kate?

For the money.

The answer came quickly. Thorson obviously enjoyed an elite lifestyle in one of the most expensive little towns in the world. The doctor could be bought. Kate might have tempted him with a fast fortune, citing Emily as the only obstacle to getting the funds in Jamison's offshore bank account.

Connor put through a call to Wellborn, who had told him that he'd be at the Denver headquarters for the FBI. He hadn't sounded happy about spending so much time with research and computers.

As soon as he answered, SAC Wellborn got right to the point. "Please tell me you have some kind of new lead."

"How about a disappearing truck, a near-fatal shooting and trace evidence of a mystery toxin?"

"Busy day."

Connor launched into a description of what had happened at the gallery and asked if the FBI could help O'Brien track the vehicles through a network of cameras.

"Send O'Brien over here," Wellborn said. "I've got a couple of techie computer guys he'd love to compare notes with. Give me more about this toxin."

Connor relayed Dr. Troutman's information. "I told him you'd be in touch."

"I'll do better than call. I'd like to go over this information in person."

"It's after five o'clock," Connor pointed out. "The doctor might not be in his office."

"Which makes it the perfect time for us to prowl around in the labs," Wellborn said. "While I'm at the hospital, I'll stop by Emily's room. I need to talk to you about her house in Aspen."

Transferring the inherited property should have been a simple matter of paperwork that Connor's assistant could handle long-distance from New York. But nothing was easy. The Riggs family lawyer was contesting her claim. "I have the property attorneys at my firm working on it. Ultimately, Emily will get what's coming to her, but it might take a while."

"And I still don't have enough evidence for a search warrant," Wellborn said.

Connor ended the call. Wellborn was right about one thing. This had been a busy day, and it wasn't over yet.

Hoping to grab a catnap, he closed his eyes. His first thought was Emily, which was getting to be standard operating procedure. Whenever he slept, he dreamed of her. This vision wasn't the usual silky, sensual image that both plagued and delighted him. In his mind, he saw her face after she'd admitted to fear. A tear spilled from her sweet blue eyes. Her lower lip trembled. He wished with all his heart that he could promise a happy ending, but that might not happen. She might never get the house in Aspen. The offshore bank account might provide proof that her ex had been an embezzler, and she'd have to face that guilt. Plus, he had a bad feeling that there would be more murder attempts.

When he heard the door open, he was surprised. He hadn't expected Emily's emergency care to be finished so quickly. His eyelids lifted, and he saw Patricia Riggs coming at him like an ancient, evil harpy. Her manicured nails were sharpened into claws.

"How dare you?" she snarled.

"Hey, Patty, have you found your fiancé?"

"Don't call me Patty. The only person who ever did was Jamison."

"And we all know what happened to him."

While she launched into a tirade about how she shouldn't be involved in any of these unseemly and terrible plots, Connor recalibrated his thinking. Patricia and Thorson might have been working together to poison Jamison with the mystery toxin. But why? The answer was, as always, money. All along, Patricia's plan might have been to inherit the Aspen house and artwork. But Jamison outsmarted her by bequeathing the property to his ex-wife. Getting Emily out of the way was the only way to make sure the property stayed in the family.

"Do you have any idea how embarrassing this is?" Patricia leaned over the recliner, literally hovering over him. "Phillip and I are staying with one of the wealthiest families in the whole damn state while we're in Denver. These are my friends—influential people. I simply can't have the local police showing up and asking to talk to me."

"Back up, Patricia."

"Why should I?"

"You have crazy eyes. You look like you're going to rip open my gut and tear out my liver."

"This is your fault. The detective you hired—that O'Brien character—sicced the cops on us. How can they think I'm a suspect in this sordid affair?"

"I asked you nicely to back up."

"I don't take orders from the likes of you, Connor Gallagher."

"You had your warning." He leaned forward, snapped the footrest down and rose in a single swift move. Though he didn't lay a hand on her, his chest bumped her.

With a shriek, she staggered back and repeated her mantra. "How dare you?"

He looked toward the door, glad to see that several of the staff stood watching this encounter. He might need witnesses. "I asked a question. Where's Thorson?"

"I don't know." She turned away from him. "I take it Emily has been attacked again."

"She was shot." Their audience in the doorway gasped in unison, and he spoke more to them than to Patricia. "But she's going to be okay."

"I left the house before the police talked to me. Do you think I should go back?"

Was she really consulting him? He couldn't believe the nerve. "Are you asking for my professional opinion?"

"I have my own lawyers," she said with a sneer.

"So I've heard. My office has been dealing with them all day. You and Phillip and probably Glenda are contesting the will, trying to keep Emily from taking possession of the property."

"It's only right," Patricia said. "If Jamison had been in his right mind, he would have left the house to his family. He loved us."

Not her. Not Phillip. There was no love lost among them. But Patricia was right about one thing. Jamison had cared deeply for his parents. Their deaths within a few months of each other—his mother from cancer and his father in a private plane crash—had shattered him. He'd been in high school, and Aunt Glenda had shipped him off to boarding school as soon as she could. He'd told Connor that he'd never forgiven his aunt. "He didn't owe you a thing."

She tossed her head, sending a ripple through her smooth brown hair. "Aunt Glenda raised him."

And she'd made it clear why she'd never had children of her own. Jamison hadn't hated her, but he'd been distant. Connor always thought that one of his attractions to Emily had been that she was—like him—without the joy that came from having a mother and father. Seen in that light, it almost made sense for him to leave the house and the art to her.

"You're not getting the house," Connor said. "Neither you nor Phillip."

"We'll see about that," she huffed. "I'm going back to Aspen to protect my interests."

"By the way…" He casually pulled the pin and dropped his grenade. When the law went his way, he thoroughly enjoyed his profession. "You and Phillip are no longer allowed in the house. Until the inheritance is settled, the doors are locked."

"You can't do that."

"Oh, but I can," he said. "If Phillip needs to remove some of his belongings, contact the sheriff's department. A deputy will accompany him."

"Where's he supposed to live?" said the woman with the nine-bedroom house.

The hospital staff who had been unabashedly watching from the doorway stepped aside as Emily was wheeled through in her chair. Connor could tell that her examination had included an extra portion of pain-killers because she actually smiled at Patricia.

"What are you doing here?" Emily's words were slurred.

"How can you be so rude? After all I've done for you?"

"You're trying to grab my inheritance." Emily's grin belied her words. "Connor says we're not going to let you. We're going to bar the door. And don't think you can sneak in the back door and steal the art, not even that small framed sketch Picasso did on a dinner napkin that I never really liked." She tapped her temple. "I have a catalog of every painting and sculpture and photo in my head. After all, I helped pick most of them out."

"These treasures belong in my family."

"Or not." Emily waved. "Goodbye, Patricia. I'll see you in Aspen."

Under her healthy tan, Patricia paled. A threatened visit from Emily scared her, and he had to wonder what she was hiding.

Chapter Fifteen

The next morning, Emily ached from so many different injuries that she couldn't pinpoint which was the worst. She didn't like to rely on medication, but the painkillers prescribed by Dr. Parris were her best friend. Those lovely pills took the edge off the hurt. And yet, she realized, the relief came at a cost. Her brain was sluggish as if she'd had a sleepless night.

She was glad to have something positive to look forward to. Today, Fish said he'd release her. She could go home to her house. Even better, Connor would be with her. Except for the bodyguards and security people, they'd have some alone time.

For the past couple of months, she and Connor had been dancing around each other with phone calls, texts and emails. They tried to connect and tentatively considered how they could get together without being too lawyer-client or too buddy-buddy or too focused on Jamison.

She exhaled a weary sigh. Relationships were hard. It had taken a handful of murder attempts to change her dynamic with Connor. Now she had a better idea of what she wanted with him. Her sigh turned into a contented purr. They definitely weren't stuck in the friend zone anymore.

She gazed across her hospital room to where he stood at the window, looking out and talking on his cell phone. She liked the way his navy sports jacket emphasized his shoulders. Connor had a lean, rangy build with narrow hips, but he wasn't skinny, and he had the don't-mess-with-me posture of a man who'd grown up scrapping with several brothers and sisters.

He ended the call and pivoted to face her where she sat in the recliner with her ankle elevated on the footrest. "Wellborn is going to stop by in a little while," he said.

"Promise not to talk to him until I get back from my physical therapy. I hope this will be my last session at the hospital."

"After that, we'll be home."

He'd said *we*, and she liked it. *They* were becoming a *we*.

"The therapist recommended some equipment I might need."

He nodded. "I passed the list to Beverly. Rehab isn't part of her job, but she knows a lot about physical conditioning. She'll work with the people at her company to take set up a minigym at your house."

"I could have handled that," she said.

"Excuse me for denying you the thrill of talking to sales departments and delivery people," he said with a full measure of sarcasm. "Nobody questions your self-reliance, Emily. You get a free pass to goof off on the day after you're shot."

"I had a bulletproof vest."

"It still counts," he said. "According to Dr. Parris, the impact of the bullet against the vest had enough force to stop your heart for thirty seconds. You were dead again."

"But I'm back." She didn't want to be dead again, not even for half a minute. "And, by the way, physical therapy can hardly be counted as goofing off."

"Agreed, and that's the kind of effort you need. You can focus on healing and getting stronger. Let me take care of the rest."

Though she knew he was right, she couldn't help being frustrated by her lack of control. This was her life. She needed to be the captain of her little ship. As the therapist helped her transfer into the wheelchair and zipped her off toward the therapy gym, Emily floated around in her muddled brain, imaging a lazy rowboat on a mountain lake. That would be her ship, and the inheritance might indicate that her ship had come in… whatever that meant.

In the physical therapy gym, she focused on the exercises, practiced walking with a cane, stretched and flexed and pedaled on a recumbent bike. Though Fish hadn't given a specific time for her departure, she hoped it would be before lunchtime, and they could order out for Chinese food. The wall clock showed it was approaching noon. She was tired and hungry and a little bit disappointed by the idea of another lunch from the hospital kitchen.

Wrapping up her exercises, she got into the wheel-chair and settled back for the ride up the elevator and down the hall to her room. With her eyelids droop-ing, she hardly noticed when the person pushing the wheelchair zipped past the three elevators and contin-ued down the hall.

"Where are we going?" she asked.

"You'll see."

The wheelchair swiveled into a room at the end of the hall. The door closed.

"Listen to me, Emily. I need to talk fast."

She looked up into the cold jade eyes of Kate Sylves-ter, who had covered her trademark red hair with a curly blond wig. For a disoriented moment, Emily wondered if she was imagining the woman who stood before her wearing aqua scrubs. "Stay away. I'll scream."

"Then you'll never hear what I have to say." Kate wheeled her to the farthest corner of the room behind the bed. "I'm guessing I have less than five minutes before your bodyguard realizes you're missing."

"Talk," Emily said.

"This has to end. Please believe me when I say that I never meant for you to be hurt. The truck banging into your car was my idea, but I never wanted him to force you off the road."

"What was your plan?"

"To make you stop and do whatever it took to con-vince you to tell me what I needed to know."

Taken aback, Emily realized that her plan made more sense than a murder attempt. "You needed me alive so you could get the bank numbers and the password."

"Jamison swore you were the only one who knew. He taunted me with how much he trusted you and claimed you were an old-fashioned note taker."

"He lied." She sat up straighter in her wheelchair and tried to get her brain to work. "He was a liar, just like you. Did you try to poison me?"

"It was a tiny dose—a pinprick. It was supposed to relax you and help you remember."

"What about the shooting yesterday?"

"That had nothing to do with me." Her hand was on the doorknob. "My partner has gone crazy, and he scares me. I'm getting the hell out of town."

"Call the police," Emily said. "Or the FBI. They'll protect you."

"Or they'll arrest me," she said darkly. "I came here to warn you. Don't go back to your house. It's dangerous. Look in the basement."

"The security people have checked it out. It's safe."

Kate whipped open the door and peered out into the hall. Over her shoulder, she said, "I loved Jamison, you know."

"Did you kill him?"

"Goodbye, Emily."

She was gone.

"No, no, no," Emily muttered to herself as she tried to get her wheelchair turned around. She couldn't let that woman escape. Even if Kate wasn't the killer, she had information that would lead to the guilty person.

Giving up on the wheelchair, Emily stood. Putting as little weight as possible on her sprained ankle, she hobbled to the door and pulled it open. At the other end of the corridor, she spotted Beverly and waved.

The bodyguard was at her side in a moment. "Where did you go?"

"Kate Sylvester was here. She grabbed my chair and zipped me down the hall before I knew what was happening."

Beverly held her shoulders and peered into her face. "Are you all right?"

"I'm fine, just feeling like an idiot. I should have been more alert."

"You need to be checked out."

She was about to protest when she remembered that Kate had admitted to giving her a shot of poison. Had there been another pinprick? She didn't want to risk another seizure. "Help me get back to the wheelchair."

As soon as she was seated, Beverly whipped her down the hall to the elevators. In seconds, she was in her room where Connor stood with Wellborn. This was a conversation Emily didn't want to miss, but her news took precedence. She spoke up. "I was just with Kate Sylvester. It was only a few minutes ago. She was wearing aqua scrubs and a blond wig."

"I'll check it out," Wellborn said. "Beverly, stay with them."

She looked up at Connor. "It might be smart for me to have some blood tests to make sure she didn't poke me with a mystery toxin."

While he put through a call to Fish, she transferred herself into the recliner chair and elevated her ankle on the footrest. If this visit from Kate messed up her chances to go home, Emily was going to be royally enraged.

"Before we go to my house," she said to Beverly, "I should tell you that Kate came to me with a warning. She said we should check in the basement, but that doesn't make sense. I don't really have a basement."

"The crawl space," Beverly said. "I'll take care of it."

Connor braced himself on the arm of her chair and leaned down to kiss her cheek. "Dr. Troutman promised to expedite the blood tests himself. How are you feeling?"

"Tired. Hungry. Light-headed from the painkillers. And really dumb for letting Kate escape."

"I heard what you told Beverly. Is that why Kate showed up? To warn you?"

Emily concentrated, trying to get past the mush in her brain and understand what had just happened. An undercurrent of emotion had given Kate's words a certain depth and significance. When she'd said that she loved Jamison, Emily sensed that she was asking for some kind of absolution. "I think she wanted me to forgive her. She said she never meant to hurt me."

"That gunshot was no accident."

"Kate claimed that she wasn't responsible for the shooting. She was working with a partner, and he had gone off the rails."

"Did she mention his name?"

She shook her head, wishing she'd done something to keep Kate in that room. "I should have knocked her unconscious with my cast. Then we'd have answers."

"I have something that'll cheer you up," he said.

"Oh, good. I need some happy thoughts before Fish rushes in here with a technician to draw more of my blood."

He went to the table beside the bed and picked up a photograph from a traffic camera. He carried it back to her and placed it in her lap. "We found the truck."

CONNOR NOTICED THE gleam in her eye as she ran her fingers over the photo of a black pickup truck with a banged-up fender on the passenger side. She cooed, "It's beautiful."

"I guess you know art."

"Artistically, it's nothing special. It's not even high resolution. But this photograph is proof that I'm not crazy. I didn't imagine the truck and freak out. I really saw it. Or did I? Where was this picture taken?"

"It came from a surveillance camera at a construction site two blocks from here."

"Yes!" She raised her good arm to cheer. "I was right! Were there other photos?"

"None that Wellborn could find." He pointed to the photo. "*See, right here.* If you look close, you can see the driver. It looks like they were wearing a baseball cap."

"It's blue." She held the photo up to her eyes and squinted. "I can't tell if it's a man or a woman. How about a license plate?"

"Not even a partial. Wellborn also did camera searches for the car with the shooter and found nothing."

Troutman charged into the room with his posse of assistants. Yesterday, Connor remembered, the doc-

tor had been enthusiastic about talking to the FBI and
being part of a real-life investigation. Today, he was
wearing a necktie with a fingerprint pattern. While he
ran through the standard examination procedures with
Emily, Connor stepped back and stood beside Beverly.

The bodyguard spoke quietly. "I wouldn't blame you
if you fired me. I wasn't paying attention. Emily was in
danger, and it was my fault."

"No need to fall on your sword," he said. "You're
not the only person to get tricked by that woman. She's
been playing all of us. Think of Wellborn. He's known
for months that Jamison's death was suspicious, but he
never got evidence."

"Was Kate involved in Jamison's death?"

Connor realized that he shouldn't be discussing mystery toxins in front of these witnesses, but the con-
nections to Jamison's death were undeniable. Kate had
admitted to poisoning Emily. Jamison could have been
her first victim. "I wouldn't be surprised if she fed him
the toxin, one bite at a time."

"She claims to be innocent."

And yet she refused to turn herself in to the police.
He wasn't ready to buy her so-called apology to Emily.
Though he didn't know Kate well, she hadn't risen to
a prestige position in a highly competitive Wall Street
investment firm by being an innocent, fluffy lamb. She
was a clever manipulator. If Jamison had been involved
in money laundering and embezzlement, Connor would
bet that Kate was right there at his side with her hand
in his pocket. She'd gone to incredible lengths to get
the account number and password.

"Bottom line," he said, "I don't trust Kate. She's the opposite of you, Beverly. I'm glad we're working together. You're loyal, moral and efficient."

"That's enough. I'm an ex-marine, not a Girl Scout."

But he wanted to let her know he liked her. Beverly wasn't the sort of woman who he felt comfortable giving a little peck on the cheek to. Shaking hands was too formal. He ripped off a salute. "I appreciate what you do."

She saluted back. "Thanks."

Troutman was just finishing up when Wellborn came back into the room. In a low voice, he said, "We caught her on camera at one of the exits, then she dashed across the street and disappeared into the neighborhood. I called in local law enforcement, but I don't expect we'll find her since I couldn't give them a model of car or license plate. And she might be a redhead or a blonde."

"She's a regular chameleon," Connor said. "Reptilian, slimy and sneaky."

"The description fits." Wellborn took off his designer sunglasses and glanced at the several people in the room. "Come with me, Connor. We'll find a place to talk, then come back here."

Two doors down, they found the necessary privacy. Connor ran through the important points Emily had told him. His greatest concern was Kate's supposedly crazy partner.

"She sounded anxious to throw him under the bus."

"Of course," Wellborn said, "she wants to divert all the guilt onto him."

"It makes sense that she has a partner. We know there

were two people in the car outside Emily's gallery—the shooter and the driver."

"Also, Kate had an alibi for the time when Emily was forced off the road. Emily was one of the first to leave Patricia's house. There had to be another person involved—the driver of the black truck."

Connor didn't know if that driver was brilliant or a complete idiot. On one hand, he'd hidden the truck so well that Deputy Sandoval and all the cops in and around Aspen couldn't find it. But then he'd driven the vehicle into Denver without fixing the dents. "We should be able to nail this guy."

"Or woman," Wellborn said grimly. "I remember my interview with Patricia and her aunt. Both of those women are capable of murder."

"They have alibis," Connor reminded him.

"I would expect them to hire an accomplice. And I can also believe that a none-too-bright accomplice wasn't supposed to cause Emily to go hurtling over the cliff."

A none-too-bright accomplice sounded a lot like Phillip, but he had an alibi. There was somebody else who fitted the bill, somebody who hadn't been at the reading of the will. "Have you located Dr. Thorson?"

"Not yet. But I've put out a BOLO. At the very least, he's a witness."

"But we can't prove anything until we have evidence."

"That's why I want to find that truck. There'll be fingerprints or trace DNA or an object left behind that will identify the driver. After that, it's game over."

When they returned to Emily's room, Dr. Troutman was waiting. He cheerfully reported that his initial analysis of Emily was positive. "We won't know if she was infected until we have the blood tests back from the lab, but she's not showing any troubling symptoms."

"And I can go home after lunch," Emily said. "Right?"

"Absolutely." He flashed her one of his brilliant smiles and then sobered as he looked toward Wellborn. "Do you have information for me?"

"I've referred the lab results you gave me to the toxicology lab at Quantico, which is one of the most advanced, well-equipped forensic facilities in the world. Now that they know what to look for, they can check this against Jamison's blood for trace elements. It'll take at least a week or more to have definitive results."

Troutman nodded. "I understand."

"I need to ask a favor, Doctor. Because we need to limit the number of people who know about this mystery toxin, I'd appreciate if you would be our point person in Denver."

"Dealing with Quantico." He couldn't hold back his grin. "I'd be honored to work with the FBI. I can tell my wife, can't I?"

"You can tell her, but no details."

"She's a mystery buff, and she's going to love this."

After Troutman left the room, Wellborn approached Emily. "We need to talk about your house in Aspen. I'm working on a legal arrangement that would designate you as the person responsible for the property before you have the deed."

Connor added to his explanation, "That means you wouldn't be able to sell the house immediately, but you could agree to open the doors to an FBI investigation without a search warrant. As soon as the paperwork is ready, you can sign."

"We'll talk about it this afternoon," she said, "after we're at my house."

Not the response he'd expected. She had every reason to advance the investigation. It didn't make sense for her to pull back. "Is there something you're not telling me?"

"I want to be there when they search. Patricia was right when she referred to the artwork as a treasure. I want to protect it. I want to be there when they search."

Another trip to Aspen wasn't his idea of a good time. And it was dangerous. As long as the killer was on the loose, Emily wasn't safe. She needed protection, not field trips. But she sounded determined. He might need to spend the rest of the day convincing her. "Before we make any plans, let's get you home."

"I can't wait. It'll be nice to have some quiet time."

He agreed. A full day of normal activity, unmarred by attempted murder, sounded like heaven.

Chapter Sixteen

Emily hobbled up the back stairs, opened the brand-new security door and entered. Inside her home, she experienced a profound sense of relief. Her tension eased, and the weight of heavy stress lifted. Her injuries seemed less painful. Being home was more effective than painkillers, with the added benefit that she wasn't dopey and disoriented.

The chaos had been tidied up, allowing her to appreciate the decorative touches she had carefully selected and placed. Living alone for the first time in her life, her home reflected her taste and no one else's. The violets on the windowsill above the kitchen sink reminded her of a kind neighbor woman who had watched her when she was a child and her mom was drunk. The sofa pillows in the front room that depicted famous paintings amused her. She'd rescued the small dining room chandelier with dangling prisms from her first New York apartment that she'd shared with two roommates. Jamison had hated that chandelier. He'd thought it was too girlie.

She felt safe in her house, even though the security

company had discovered not one but two explosive devices in the crawl space. She owed Kate a thank-you for the warning. Destroying her charming little house would have been a shame.

At the foot of the staircase, she paused.

Connor stepped up beside her. "Can I give you a lift?"

Though she thoroughly enjoyed being carried in his arms, the physical therapist had been working with her on stairs. "I want to try it myself, but I'd like for you to follow close behind in case I get tired or stumble over my own feet."

"You won't trip," he said. "You've been walking like a champ. We brought the wheelchair just in case, but you're doing fine with the cane."

"Thank you for getting the place put back together."

"I can't take credit. Beverly's employers contacted the cleaning crew. They specialize in crime scenes."

"Don't tell me more. I have enough grisly details of my own to think about."

She slowly ascended the staircase, leaning on the banister and not putting too much weight on her ankle. With the compression wrap, the injury hardly looked swollen. But she still felt the tightness. The therapist had warned her about not doing too much and frequently repeated the acronym for the care of a sprain: RICE. It stood for *Rest*, *Ice*, *Compression* and *Elevation*. Rest was probably the most important.

She made it into her bedroom, sat on the edge of her bed and ran her hand across her clean white duvet with the eyelet trim. Connor followed. Like her, he seemed more relaxed. He'd taken off his sports jacket, and the sleeves of his blue oxford cloth shirt were rolled up to the elbows. Though there were other people in the house, she felt like they were alone. They had no pressing need to talk about the investigation or her physical condition or any other kind of business. In this moment, it was only the two of them.

Kicking off her shoes, she scooted around on the bed until her back was supported by pillows and her legs stretched out in front of her. Though comfortable enough, she didn't like this position. "I'm not really a bed person. I don't like breakfast in bed, don't like to lie around. If I read in bed, I just fall asleep. But I know that I need to rest."

He went to the west-facing window and pulled up the shade, allowing the afternoon light to spill across the small square table with a center drawer and matching blond wood chairs on each end. "We could bring a comfortable chair up here."

"I don't have one with a built-in footrest." She didn't want to turn her bedroom into a replica of her hospital room, but she needed somewhere to sit where she could put her leg up. And a breakfast table might be nice.

"There are places that rent chairs like that."

"I definitely don't need more furniture in the house," she said. "Where did Beverly put the exercise equipment?"

"Guest bedroom. With the recumbent bike, the step machine and a couple of other contraptions, there isn't much room for the bed."

"Beverly did a good job setting up my home gym. But where will you sleep?"

A slow, sexy grin stretched the corners of his mouth. "I'll figure something out."

She had a couple of her own ideas on the interrelated subjects of where he should go to bed and how she should get her exercise. There were lots of creative ways they could get hot and sweaty together, and she wouldn't mind trying them out.

With a quick knock, Beverly and the part-time nurse entered her bedroom. Protection was her bodyguard's primary concern. She outlined the security systems that were currently in place, including an alarm system and hidden cameras. An additional bodyguard would be on duty downstairs. Beverly preferred to have Emily stay on the second floor because there was only one way to get up there—the staircase.

The part-time nurse chimed in. She seemed nice enough but had a singsong voice. When she started listing reasons why her patient shouldn't be climbing up and down the stairs, Emily's interest faded. She was tired. All she really wanted was dinner and a nap.

Connor read her mind. He herded everyone else from the room and sat beside her on the bed. "How about a bath?"

"Oh, I hadn't even thought about that, but it sounds great. A bubble bath."

He led the way into the white-tiled bathroom adjoining her bedroom, and he locked the other door that opened onto the second floor. When he turned on the water in the tub, he commented approvingly, "Massaging water jets. Nice."

"This was the only room I remodeled when I moved in. The toilet converts into a bidet, the shower can be used as a sauna and the tub, well, the tub is wonderful."

He helped her take the compression wrap off her ankle and brought in extra towels—fluffy lavender and yellow—to rest her casted left arm upon. Though he was more than willing to stay with her, Emily threw him out. His assistance was not required to get undressed, and removing the bulletproof vest and the wrap around her ribs was the furthest thing from a sexy striptease. She didn't want him to think of her as a patient.

She added scented bubble bath to the swirling water and carefully climbed into the tub. The hot water and massaging jets were sheer bliss. With a moan of pleasure, she lay back, closed her eyes and let the pulsating water soothe her battered body. She hadn't indulged in a luxurious bath like this in quite a while. There never seemed to be time. Her gallery kept her busy. When the attacks were over and her life returned to normal, she vowed to take advantage of this fantastic tub on a more regular basis.

There was a tap on the door. Connor peeked inside and said, "I brought you an iced mint tea."

Her favorite! She arranged the bubbles so nothing was showing. "Come in."

He carried a tray with her tall glass of tea and a plate of sliced peaches, and he placed it on a towel on the floor. "Fresh-picked fruit from the trees by your driveway."

Kneeling beside the tub, his eyes were level with

hers. Neither of them looked away. They'd waited nearly a decade for this privacy and intimacy. She knew him so well.

His gaze lowered and lingered on her wet, bare shoulders and arms. He cleared his throat. His voice was hoarse. "I should go."

"Wait," she said. "Would you set up some candles for me? In the second drawer by the sink, there are votive containers and matches."

He did as she asked, lighting the flames on half a dozen candles, which he placed around the bathroom. "They smell good."

"Now I want you to pull down the shade." She sipped her iced tea and licked her lips. "Now turn out the light."

The bathroom wasn't pitch-dark. A bit of sunlight crept around the edge of the shade. But the flickering illumination of candlelight created an atmosphere of warm sensuality. Shadows outlined his brow and cheekbones. He hadn't shaved since her first day in the hospital, and his stubble was heavy.

In a barely audible whisper, she said, "Now take off your shirt."

Apparently, he heard her loud and clear because he unfastened the buttons with lightning speed. The shirt was gone. She wanted to run her fingers through the swath of dark hair on his chest, but her cast was in the way. Trying to get her right arm into position, she twisted in the tub. A sharp jab in her torso reminded her that her ribs were injured. Nonetheless, she tried again. The bubbly, scented water splashed and churned.

"Let me help," he said.

"Try not to get the casts wet."

He reached into the water, leveraged his hands under her arms and lifted her up and out. Water streamed from her body as he placed her on the edge of the tub.

"I know what you're doing." She pushed her wet hair off her forehead. "You just want to see me without my clothes."

"I could give you a towel."

He crouched in front of her, still holding her upper arms so she wouldn't lose her balance and topple backward. His gaze was brazen and demanding as he stared at her naked body. She should have been embarrassed. But she liked the effect her nudity was having on him.

Shoulders back and chin lifted, she stared back at him. "I don't want a towel."

"You're beautiful, Emily."

He wasn't half-bad himself. "The first time I saw you, I had second thoughts about Jamison. I've always—"

"Stop." He placed a finger across her lips. "Let's not talk about the past. I want to start working on a future, our future."

Turned sideways, she embraced him. His bare chest rubbed against her slippery, wet breasts as his arms encircled her. Their lips joined.

As their kiss deepened, their position changed. She slid against him. He lifted her. Their arms tangled and somehow she found herself lying on a towel on the tile floor.

"I'll try to be careful," he said. "Tell me if I hurt you."

She was willing to put up with a little pain for what she imagined would be a great deal of pleasure. He trailed soft kisses down her neck, where he nuzzled and nibbled. He took a sharp nip at her throat, and she gave a startled yelp.

Immediately, he backed off.

"Don't stop," she said. "I'm not hurt."

He rose above her, supporting himself on his elbows and knees. She could tell that he was trying not to put too much weight on her, and she appreciated his concern. But she didn't want to be treated like she was helpless.

She pressed her good hand against his chest. "I have an idea."

"I'm listening."

Her index finger trailed down the center of his chest, following the line of dark hair until she tugged at his belt. "Take off the rest of your clothes and lie down. I'll be on top."

He bolted to his feet and stripped off his belt and jeans. After he stretched out on the floor, she braced herself against him. At first, she took her time. With her right hand, she traced light circles on his chest and torso.

She straddled him, and then lowered herself so they were touching from head to toe. His body absorbed the moisture from hers. She kissed him with the passion she'd suppressed for all these years when they were friends, only friends. Her tongue plunged into his mouth. Her fingernails scraped against his skin. How had she found the courage to be so aggressive? Maybe it had something to do with being near death on a regular basis.

She wanted him and couldn't hold back. Instead of

a slow, subtle seduction, she was all over him. Her arm cast made her clumsy, but he wasn't complaining. His erection pressed against her. She wanted him inside her.

"Emily, slow down. We need a condom."

"Don't you have one?" Nearly overwhelmed by need, she sucked down a huge lungful of air. Her chest heaved. "What are you saying?"

"We have to stop."

"No." She stared down into his dark eyes and shook her head. How could she control this hunger? "I want you."

"Oh, baby, I want you, too."

He held her face in both hands and kissed her hard. A fierce need throbbed through her veins. With a groan, she collapsed onto his chest.

He held her there. His hand slipped between them and descended her body, gliding past her stomach to the juncture of her widespread thighs. His fingers massaged her sex, accelerated her nascent passion to an unbearable level. He fulfilled her.

She rolled off him, not apologizing when her cast bumped his chest. She still wanted the full treatment, but she was happy with what he'd given her. Sensual tremors radiated outward from her groin. Her pulse raced at an urgent speed. "That was good."

"I know."

She wanted to believe there would be plenty of time for them to further this relationship and have even more sex, but the constant murder attempts reminded her that life was fragile. She needed to seize every opportunity that presented itself. She doubted there would ever be another man who was as right for her as Connor.

He lurched to his feet and gathered his clothes. "I'll help you get dressed."

"I'm not ready to move." She wanted to savor the thrill. "You go. I'll be out in a minute."

In spite of the great orgasm, she was a little bit mad at him. He should have been prepared. Wasn't it a man's duty to carry a condom at all times? She supposed it could be argued that a woman had the same responsibility. Really, it was nobody's fault.

Taking her time, she brushed her teeth, used a blow-dryer on her hair and put on makeup for the first time in days. She slipped into a silky pink robe with kimono sleeves. When she was done, she looked through the window. The sun had gone down, and the streetlights were glowing. Almost time for bed, and she wondered if he would join her under the covers. If so, he'd better have a condom with him.

When she stepped into her bedroom, she saw that a minor transformation had taken place. A chaise longue from her living room had been moved up here. It was an old-fashioned design but actually comfortable and perfect for elevating her ankle. The table beside it was the perfect height for her to recline and dine. On the table, a fresh glass of tea awaited her along with a big green salad and a slice of pepperoni pizza.

Connor took her arm to escort her. "Dinner."

Pizza from Luciano's was a treat, and she didn't want to be ungrateful. But it was irritating that he hadn't asked her before placing the order...or moving her furniture around. If he was Mr. Prepared, why hadn't he thought ahead and bought condoms?

She arranged herself on the chaise. "I want to get my ankle wrapped before the nurse leaves for the night."

"I'll get her," Connor said. "She put the pills you'll need before bed into this paper cup on the dresser."

Before he went out the door, she spoke up. "Listen, Connor, I appreciate everything you're doing, but I don't want you to get the wrong idea."

"Explain."

"You're making all the phone calls and arrangements, hiring people to take care of me, rearranging my furniture and you even ordered dinner without asking me what I want. Never mind that pizza is probably what I would have ordered. I want to make my own decisions."

"I understand."

"This is important. I don't want you to think you're running the show."

He forgot about calling the nurse and took a seat on the other side of the table. His expression was serious. "Don't confuse me with your ex-husband. I know what Jamison was like. He was a master manipulator. He's been dead for months, and he's still got us jumping through hoops."

"I would never confuse you with him."

"When I do things for you, it's not because I'm trying to control you," he said. "I want to support you in doing what you want."

She took a sip of her iced tea and cocked her head to one side. This might be the right time to test his motivations. "I want to get this straight. You are not trying to control me."

"Not at all."

"Suppose I said I wanted to go to Aspen, to be there when the FBI searches the house. Would you be okay with that?"

He threw up his hands. "That's not a fair question."

"Why not? Is it because you don't think I'll like the answer?"

"It's not safe for you to go there," he said. "Here, in your house, you're protected. Nobody is going to get in here and hurt you. I don't want you to take the risk."

"That's not your decision, Connor." She'd made her point, but the victory was hollow. "I don't want to argue with you. There are so many other ways—better ways—we can use our time."

The air in the room seemed to vibrate. In an instant, everything changed. There was a massive explosion. The windows rattled in their frames.

Chapter Seventeen

Connor rushed to the window at the front of her bedroom. The explosion had come from that direction, and his first instinct had been to confront the danger and protect Emily. He raised the window shade and looked past the tree branches to the street outside her house. At the curb, a vehicle was on fire. Fingers of yellow flame clawed their way across the hood and roof. Smoke gushed. There were other cars on the street. He didn't see any witnesses.

Beverly charged into the room. "Step back from the windows," she ordered. "Standing there in the light, you make a clear target."

"What's going on?" Emily asked.

"I'm guessing it was a car bomb."

He pivoted to face the bodyguard. "It was the truck, wasn't it? The black truck."

"We won't know until the police investigate."

Already a chorus of sirens from fire trucks and police cruisers echoed through the night. Emily's house was near central Denver, and response time was quick. Connor wanted to run downstairs and tell the cops that this fire wasn't an accident. They needed to fan out and start a search, question witnesses, check cameras. They had to find him…or her…whatever. They had to arrest this psycho. Blowing up the truck in front of Emily's house was a choreographed attack, designed to send a message. The psycho was thumbing his or her nose at them.

Connor strode toward the exit, but Beverly blocked his way. "Stand down," she said. "Let the police do their job."

"I could help."

"You need to stay here and take care of Emily. Don't go near the windows. I'll let you know as soon as I have information."

She closed the door behind her.

Emily remained on the chaise with her ankle elevated on a pillow. "I don't get it," she said. "Why blow up the truck?"

"Potential evidence."

"Of course! The dents on the bumper were proof that I was run off the road. And there were probably fingerprints."

"The fire will obliterate any trace," he said. "Unless the police pick up Kate Sylvester and she agrees to talk or confesses, we've got nothing."

The trip to Aspen became even more imperative. The house that had belonged to Jamison was the last, best place to uncover any sort of clues. Connor had already made plans to go there tomorrow with Wellborn. The only question was whether they'd drive or take a police helicopter.

The commotion from the street in front of her house

grew louder and more chaotic. It took willpower to keep from going to the window and watching the fire department in action. The smoke—a stinking combination of gasoline and burning rubber—permeated the air. From downstairs, he heard doors slamming and loud conversations. The alarm hadn't gone off, so Beverly must have given the okay for someone to enter.

He had his hand on the doorknob, ready to find out who was in the house, when Emily spoke up. "Connor, wait. You were told to stand down."

"I'm not a recruit in Beverly's army. She doesn't get to give me orders."

"Believe me," she said, "I understand how you're feeling. Nobody likes being on the sidelines, but there's nothing you can do. If they need you, they know where to find you."

"You're right," he said.

"I know."

"Don't gloat."

He returned to the chair opposite her chaise. For lack of anything better to do, he folded the pizza slice and took a bite. The twirling red and blue lights from emergency vehicles flashed against the window. He was dying to rush outside and join them.

"There must be other evidence," she said. "Ballistics on the bullets they used?"

"They need a weapon for comparison."

"How about this?" she said. "Wellborn said that his tech guys didn't find anything when they hacked into my computer files, but they aren't me. If I could take a look at the stuff they've dug up, I might notice something."

"Can't hurt," he said. "I'll arrange for someone to come here."

"I could go to the local FBI headquarters, unless you think it's better for me to sit here and do nothing."

Her smile had an ironic twist. He knew what sort of game she was playing. By comparing her situation with his, she intended to show him that he was being unreasonable. "You're not real subtle," he said.

"It doesn't matter as long as I'm convincing."

She wiggled her eyebrows, and he noticed that she was wearing makeup that made her eyes even more blue and beautiful. Her streaked blond hair covered the bruise and stitches on her forehead. She looked strong, healthy and full of energy.

"If you didn't have that cast on your arm," he said, "I wouldn't know you were in a car crash. You're healing fast."

"I still have bruises."

He had just seen every delicious inch of her body, and he thought she looked good. "The worst is the area near your shoulder, where the bullet hit."

"Tomorrow," she said, circling back to the topic, "I can stop by the FBI offices. Or I could go to Aspen."

Or none of the above. He couldn't order her what to do and couldn't physically restrain her, but he refused to put her in a dangerous situation. Her house was well protected. She needed to stay here.

Beverly came into the room. "It's going to be tough to figure out who owns the truck. The VIN number and all the other identifiers have been removed."

"No surprise," he said. "What else?"

Her lips pinched together. "There was someone inside. A woman. There's not much left of her, not enough for immediate identification."

"Kate Sylvester," Emily whispered. "That's a heinous way to die. She didn't deserve it."

Connor wasn't so sure. Kate sure as hell deserved some form of punishment. She'd admitted having been involved in the attacks on Emily, and it was likely that she'd administered the mystery toxin that killed Jamison. He remembered seeing her on Jamison's arm at cocktail parties and events. They'd been a dazzling couple. Now both were dead. The ill-gotten money in the offshore bank account—no matter how much— wasn't worth this cost.

THE NEXT DAY, Emily felt better, even considering everything that had happened. After consulting with the nurse, she'd reduced her painkiller dosage to just a little more than aspirin. And her emotional wellness was improved, having been given a substantial boost after last night in bed with Connor, who had been resourceful enough to rustle up three condoms. They used them all. In future, she thought, they should consider buying in bulk.

For the first time in days, her mind was clear. She could see that the obstacles to taking charge of her life were of her own making. Connor told her—emphatically—that he didn't want her to leave the protection of her house, and he was entitled to that opinion. He didn't dictate her actions and didn't control her life. Whatever happened, it was her decision.

Sitting downstairs at the dining table with the prism

chandelier casting shards of sunlight around the room, she gazed at the man who had been her friend for a very long time and was now something more. Before he'd come to her bed last night, he'd shaved. Though the stubble was trendy, she liked his smooth, stubborn chin. Sipping her coffee, she said, "I've decided not to sign Wellborn's document. Unless you take me along, the FBI doesn't have my permission to search the Aspen house."

"Fine."

She'd expected more resistance. "I'm serious."

He dug into the cheese omelet that he'd served up moments ago with bagels on the side. Since everybody in the house was on a different schedule, they cooked and ate whenever convenient. "You can tell Wellborn yourself. He ought to be here in a couple of minutes. Then I'm leaving with him. We're taking a police chopper."

"You're still going to Aspen? But you can't get into the house."

"I'm a lawyer, and he's a fed." Connor shrugged. "We'll figure out something."

She stabbed the yellow omelet with her fork. Just like that! Her leverage was gone. They could work around her, and she couldn't force them to take her along by withholding her signature. "Smooth move."

"Whatever you might think, I'm not trying to manipulate you. I have concerns about your safety, and I don't want to put you at risk."

"It's my choice whether I crochet doilies or swim with sharks."

He reached across the table and took her hand. "I care about you, Emily. So do plenty of other people. After the explosion last night, your phone has been ringing nonstop."

She frowned. "How do you know? My cell phone was lost in the crash."

"These calls are on your landline. People left dozens of messages. Last night, Beverly worried that the entire mariachi band would show up on the doorstep, so she talked to one of your part-time employees, Julia."

"Julia Espinoza. She's a terrific help."

"She agreed to get the word out, and suggested you get a new cell phone as soon as possible."

The outpouring of concern touched her. "The mariachis were coming here?"

"And a mob of artists and your book club and more." He gave her fingers a squeeze. "They care. And I care. That means you have a responsibility to us. We don't want to lose you."

He was persuasive. Perhaps Connor was manipulating her, but she was beginning to think that she should do as he suggested. His concern seemed sincere. But so was her desire to take charge and do things for herself.

Wellborn arrived, cool and collected as always. After asking Beverly to join them, he sat at the end of the table. "Here's the update," he said. "We know the year, make and model of the truck. None of our suspects own a vehicle that matches the description. Deputy Sandoval suggested that it might be stolen, although the sheriff's department hasn't received a report for a missing truck."

Emily had an explanation, "People who don't live

full-time in the mountains might leave a vehicle behind while they aren't at their home, especially a truck."

Wellborn continued, "We believe the body in the truck was Kate Sylvester. It'll take a while for DNA analysis and reconstruction, but she was carrying a passport in a silver case that protected it from the explosion."

Emily pushed away the mental image of a body that had been burned so badly it couldn't be recognized. Only a few hours earlier, she'd spoken to Kate.

Connor said, "Our main suspect seems to be Phillip. Does he have an alibi for last night?"

"He claimed that he was on the road, driving back home to Aspen. His sister was with him."

Not a very solid alibi in Emily's opinion. Phillip and Patricia wouldn't hesitate to lie for each other. "What about her fiancé?"

"I haven't been able to reach Dr. Thorson." He set his briefcase on the table, popped open the lid and took out a document. "If you'll sign these papers, Emily, we'll be on our way."

She made one last attempt. "I'd like to be with you when the house is opened."

Wellborn glanced at Connor, who looked down and shook his head. His gesture irritated her far more than his rationalizations. She really didn't like the way these two men were deciding the limits for her. Now was the time to do a *carpe diem* and take matters into her own hands. She had a plan, and it didn't include them. Without a word, she picked up the pen and signed on the line where Wellborn had marked an X.

The lawyer and the fed could do whatever necessary. And she would do the same.

After Connor had left with Wellborn, she moved forward, confident that she could handle the arrangements. Taking a landline phone to her bedroom, she closed the door and got busy. Using various friends and contacts, it had taken her less than an hour to schedule her own helicopter flight to Aspen, hiring a charter service that she and Jamison had used before. The hard part was convincing Beverly. After much debate, she worked out a compromise, allowing Beverly to accompany her.

Walking with her cane, Emily boarded a motor home driven by an artist friend who was somewhat paranoid and had outfitted his home on wheels like a fortress. Beverly approved of the triple-pane windows, reinforced walls and four guns stashed in various places. It seemed to Emily that Beverly also liked the artist, who was six feet seven inches tall and built like Paul Bunyan. The bodyguard sat in the passenger seat as they drove south to a private airfield, pulled onto the tarmac and parked outside hangar fourteen, where a red-and-white helicopter was tethered. So far, her trip to Aspen was working out precisely as planned.

When she climbed out of the motor home and walked toward the chopper, a tall blond man wearing a down vest and sunglasses came toward her, moving fast. He enveloped her in a bear hug that was much too familiar and much too tight.

"Great to see you," he said.

She pulled her head back. "Do I know you?"

"I'm the guy who saved your life." A hard-edged object poked at her injured ribs. "It's me. Eric. You remember. Dr. Eric Thorson."

Chapter Eighteen

Emily had never actually seen Dr. Thorson. While in his care, she'd been in a coma. Twisting her arm, she struggled to escape his grasp. "Get away from me."

"Don't fight it. You're coming with me." Still holding her with one hand, he faced Beverly and the artist. Thorson held open his vest to show them an array of explosives attached to the inner lining. "Gunnery Sergeant T. J. Beverly, with your military experience, I believe you're familiar with suicide vests."

Another bomb. Emily's heart jumped into her throat. She couldn't scream if she wanted to. Escape with her sprained ankle was impossible. She'd organized herself into an ambush.

"Nobody has to get hurt," Beverly said.

"Exactly what I'm thinking," Thorson said. "In my left hand, I'm holding the kill switch. As long as I keep this button pressed down, we've got no problem. But if I release—because maybe you shot me—we'll all be blown sky-high. Just like the truck last night."

Beverly said, "I won't let you hurt Emily."

"Not my intention. All I'm after is information. As

soon as she tells me what I need to know, she's free to go. Simple."

Drawing on a reservoir of courage she never knew she had, Emily squared her shoulders. "It's all right, Beverly. I'll go with him."

"Good girl." Still holding the kill switch in his left hand, Thorson wrapped his right arm around her midsection and pulled her backward to the helicopter.

When Beverly started toward them, he waggled the kill switch. "Don't move."

Inside the chopper, he shoved Emily toward the rear and pulled his handgun, which he aimed at a gray-haired man, who was handcuffed to a metal strut. His name was Steve; she recognized him from a few years ago. "I'm so sorry," she said to him. "I had no idea this would happen."

"My fault," he muttered. "I let this jerk get the drop on me."

"No need for name-calling," Thorson said as he tossed Emily a set of keys. "Unfasten his cuffs. We need to take off."

After she unlocked the cuffs and the pilot moved forward to his seat, Thorson sat in the copilot position. He directed her to sit in a seat behind the pilot so he could keep an eye on both of them.

Through the windshield, she watched Beverly, who was gesturing emphatically and talking on her cell phone. Who could she call? Who could possibly change this turn of events?

"Let's go," Thorson said. "I want to get the hell out of here."

When the pilot turned the ignition, the engine roared and the rotor slashed through the air. It was too loud to talk, but she had to have some answers.

"How did you know?" she shouted. "How did you know I was going to be here?"

"You can thank Kate for that," he yelled back. "When she visited you at the hospital, she attached a bug. Over the past couple of days, I've been listening to every word you said."

"Impossible." There was nowhere Kate could have hidden a bug. Emily had changed clothes several times. She'd been naked and washed her hair. "Where did she hide this bug?"

He reached over with the gun and tapped her cast. "She slipped it in here. Call it microtechnology. It's tiny, miniscule. You never even felt it, did you?"

She'd had an itch but nothing painful, nothing compared to the wrenching agony in her gut when she'd realized that Thorson had been listening to her intimate conversations with Connor. That violation disgusted her more than she could ever express in words. Seething with impotent anger, she jammed her finger into the cast and dug around at the edges until she found the tiny disk. She ripped out the microtechnology, threw it on the floor of the chopper and crushed it with her foot as they lifted off.

Swooping through clear blue skies toward the mountains west of town, she tamped down her rage. It wouldn't do any good to explode. More than ever before, she had to play this smart. "Where are you taking me?" she yelled.

"None of your business," he said. "It's going to be a nice, smooth ride. I've explained to the pilot about the kill switch. And he's not going to be putting through any calls to airfields. We're on our own."

She didn't know how the airborne communication systems worked but was certain that Beverly would have alerted authorities. Someone would be tracking them. Thorson was seriously delusional if he thought he could get away with this.

He manipulated the mechanics on his kill switch so he could set it aside without triggering an explosion. Then he passed her noise-canceling headphones with an attached microphone so they could talk to each other without yelling. Still keeping the gun aimed at her, he handed her two other items: her computer and her cell phone.

She clenched her jaw when she saw the laptop and her battered phone. "Did you grab these when my car crashed?"

"That wasn't supposed to happen." His voice was easier to hear over the headset. "I barely nudged your car. If you weren't such a bad driver, you could have kept it on the road. Kate and I could have asked questions then, and none of this would have happened. I never intended to hurt you."

She pressed her lips together to keep from shooting off her mouth and telling him that he wasn't making sense. Logic told her that he and Kate would have killed her when they had what they wanted. But it wouldn't do any good to quibble with a psycho.

He continued, "Open your laptop and check your documents."

"I can't believe they still work."

"And they still get internet. Find me the name of the bank and the password."

He didn't need the account number. Kate had already got that from the iguana photo in her bedroom.

"Dr. Thorson." She addressed him using his title, hoping to remind him that he was more than a mindless thug. He was an ER doctor and virologist. "You must know that the FBI already hacked into my laptop. They didn't find a list of passwords."

"They weren't familiar with Jamison the way you were. Kate was sure you knew."

"And look where it got her."

She watched him for a reaction. He'd admitted to blowing up the truck, and he certainly knew about the woman inside. The expression in his slate blue eyes was unreadable. She couldn't tell if he was sad or angry or just plain confused. What was his relationship with Kate?

"I'll miss her."

But he must have killed her. "I understand. You have regrets."

"Shut the hell up."

Don't poke the bear. Long ago, her mom had offered that advice when Emily wouldn't stop teasing one of the guys she was dating. When he'd hauled back his meaty fist and smacked Emily, Mom gloated and told her that she deserved to be hit. Just like now. Emily should have stayed at her house.

Looking out the side window, she saw that they'd left the densely packed houses of Denver behind. The chopper seemed to be following the route of a highway, winding deeper into the foothills.

She guessed the trip to Aspen would be a little over an hour. Was Aspen their destination? If they went to the house, Connor and Wellborn would be there. Somebody might be able to stop Thorson.

"I loved her," Thorson mumbled. "Kate was beautiful and smart. When we accessed the funds in the offshore account, we would have had enough money to disappear and live like royalty for the rest of our lives."

"But you were engaged to Patricia."

"That was over. She found me and Kate together. You know, doing it."

Emily had lived a similar scene. She had to wonder if Kate engineered these moments when a wife or girlfriend would walk in and catch her having sex with their husband or lover. Kate was competitive. Stealing another woman's man probably gave her a thrill.

"She wanted to turn herself in," Thorson said. "I told her it was crazy, that we'd end up in jail, but she wouldn't listen. We argued. I was so damn mad. I went storming off. That's the last time I saw her alive."

She noticed that he hadn't confessed to murder. "Then what happened?"

"That's all I'm going to say. You start reading the documents."

"What if I can't find anything?"

"We move to plan B. You and I go to the bank in the Caymans and use your fingerprints to withdraw all the money in that account."

There was no way in hell she'd allow that to happen. Thorson sickened her. She'd almost rather die than go to the Caymans with him. "I'll find something."

With her laptop balanced on her knees, she brought up the familiar screen with her many icons and documents. There was one icon she'd been thinking about from the first moment she heard about her inheritance. Before they had broken up, Jamison had created a file on her computer that contained photos of all the artwork they'd purchased.

She clicked, and it opened. The screen showed a remarkable Kandinsky abstract. She flipped through the pictures—not sure of what she was looking for, but knowing there was something important hidden in those works. Most of their art collection was modern or postmodern, but she paused on a painting by an unknown artist who painted in the style of Edward Hopper. Not a particularly brilliant picture, but there was a haunting loneliness to the scene of a young woman sitting at a desk in front of a window with bleak gray light shining down on her hands as she wrote. The title of the painting was *The Note Taker*.

Emily remembered that Kate had referred to her as a note taker. Jamison had made that comparison as well, teasing her about her notebook, where she wrote down reminders rather than keeping them on her computer.

"I've got the answer," she said. "We need to go to Aspen."

"Tell me why."

She explained about the painting. "Do you remember how Jamison wrote the number for the bank account on the photo that I hung in my bedroom? Well, I think he did the same thing with a painting in Aspen. It's called *The Note Taker.*"

When she held up her laptop so he could see the picture, he laughed out loud. "I've walked past this picture a million times. Your ex-husband was a crafty bastard. I guess we have to go to Aspen."

While he was distracted by talking to the pilot, she turned on her phone. With only one bar left, it was almost out of power. Even with her clumsy right hand, she managed a quick text to Connor's phone: J's Aspen home. ETA: 1 hr.

Though unsure of what Connor could do, she trusted him. The realization struck her with belated force. *Trust!* It had always been an issue with her, and she deeply, honestly trusted him more than any other person in her life. Even in the early years of their marriage, she hadn't felt this way about Jamison. Her mother had never been in the least trustworthy. Connor was different. He found ways to protect her. He'd stayed at her bedside, had hired a security firm with a bodyguard and had advised her to stay safe at home today. She should have listened to him.

Okay, sure, she'd made wrong decisions, but she wasn't about to give up. She wouldn't let Thorson win.

Somehow, she had to figure out a way to deal with his suicide vest. Or did she? Was he really crazy enough to detonate the device, killing himself and everyone else around him? She knew he didn't want to be taken into custody, but death was a terrible solution.

She considered physical action. No way could she overpower him. The doctor was a big athletic man who could pick her up and bounce her off the windows of the chopper without breaking a sweat. There might be something she could do to separate him from the explosives. Right now, he had manipulated the kill switch so it was deactivated. Could she grab the switch and throw it from the chopper? Not likely—he wouldn't let her near the switch.

If not physically overpowering him, she had to convince him to let them go. To open a dialogue, she asked, "Where did you learn about explosives?"

"I did an internship in western Africa, where militants were fighting the established order. One of the rebels took a shine to me. I wasn't involved with his cause, but I learned about firearms and explosives."

"Is Africa where you studied virology?"

"I wish I'd never learned about those poisons and diseases."

The pilot interrupted, "Excuse me, but the way I understand the doctor's instructions is fly to the house where I used to take Emily and Jamison."

"That's right," she said. "What was your prior destination?"

"He doesn't exactly know," Thorson said. "I have a

hideout near Glenwood. My plan was to have you give me the numbers, go there and transfer the money from the offshore account to another untraceable account that Kate set up for me."

She had a feeling that Kate had been the one who plotted and made plans. "What were you going to do with us?"

"I'd go on the run and disappear. And I'd let you go free." He focused on her. "Pay attention, Emily. I told you before, I'm not a killer."

Even if she accepted his excuse for running her off the road, there were other incidents. "What about messing with my medication when I was in a coma? And giving Kate something to infect me in Denver? And shooting me?"

"The stuff with the meds never put you in danger. As for the shooting? Not me."

Why should she believe him? "What about Kate's death?"

"God, no, I didn't hurt her. I stormed off after our fight. When I came back, she was dead. Shot with impressive skill through the heart."

"And then you put her in the truck?"

"We'd already discussed blowing up the truck to erase the evidence, and I decided it would be her funeral pyre. Like for a warrior princess. It seemed appropriate. She deserved a fierce send-off."

Emily found herself buying into his story. She desperately wanted to believe that Thorson would allow her and Steve, the pilot, to go free. "If you really haven't committed murder, you should take Kate's advice and turn yourself in. The FBI might even make a deal with you in exchange for information about Jamison's account."

"They've got stuff to charge against me. I didn't kill him, but I provided the toxin Kate administered to your ex-husband over a period of months. I always thought he'd recover, but I was wrong. That makes me an accessory—a common criminal. Also, if I turn myself in, I'll be flat broke. And they sure as hell won't let me practice medicine."

She had to agree that his future sounded bleak. Her arguments weren't doing much to change his mind.

Her cell phone, which she'd left turned on, trilled. She looked down at the screen. Caller ID showed it was Connor. She held it so Thorson could see. Without asking his permission, she answered.

"Connor, it's Emily. You're on speaker. We can all hear you."

"Thorson," Connor said. "If you plan to come to the house in Aspen, we need to make arrangements so nobody will accidentally shoot you and blow up the chopper."

"I want a deal," Thorson said. "I want to talk to the FBI agent."

"We can do that."

"I don't want to set off another explosion." Thorson's smile was cold. "But if I don't get what I want, somebody is going to die."

Emily shuddered. That threat sounded more honest than anything Thorson had said before. Maybe he actually was innocent of murder, but she sensed that he'd do what he deemed necessary. If that meant she and Steve got blown sky-high, so be it.

Chapter Nineteen

The red-and-white helicopter piloted by the grand-fatherly man named Steve hovered outside the spectacular mansion Emily had inherited. Such a beautiful setting, the meadow property was surrounded by forest and vistas of distant snowcapped peaks. She had enjoyed much of the time she'd spent here with Jamison—the long hikes, watching the sunset behind the Rockies, wading in the creek that ran through the property. The downside was the unfortunate proximity to his family.

"You struck it rich," Thorson muttered.

Though she couldn't bear to live in a house paid for by illegal schemes that hurt the investor, she had to admit that the house was remarkable. "The best part is the artwork inside. I snagged a couple of true masterpieces."

As the chopper descended on the flat area to the south of the house, she looked around for the police helicopter. It was nowhere in sight. Nor did she see police cruisers. Thorson had taken the phone for a private conversation with Connor, so she didn't exactly know what they had worked out.

"Where is everybody?" she asked.

"No cops," he said. "I told Connor. No cops."

"I thought you were going to turn yourself in."

"I haven't decided, but I knew for sure that I didn't want to take a chance on some trigger-happy deputy shooting me while I walk up to the house."

"Neither do I." If Thorson was shot and took his thumb off the kill switch, they'd all die, unless… "Are you still going to be wearing the suicide vest?"

He frowned. "Connor didn't want me to, but I need the insurance."

The chopper landed, kicking up a curtain of dry dirt and leaves. She peered through the window and saw Connor approaching. Alone, he walked without hesitation, showing no fear. Not many men would take this kind of risk, and it was especially unexpected from an attorney from Brooklyn. He wasn't trained to fight psychos and didn't even know how to handle a gun, but he stepped up.

She was grateful and proud of her man.

Did he know how much she valued him? Did he realize how the passion they had shared last night had deepened their connection? She hadn't told him that she loved him. Instead, she'd got up this morning with a chip on her shoulder, demanding to take care of herself. Her self-reliance wasn't wrong, and she wouldn't apologize for it. But she also trusted him.

By the time the rotors stopped churning, Thorson had the kill switch reengaged and clutched in his left hand. The gun was in his right. He nodded to her. "Open the door."

Connor climbed inside. His gaze fixed on her. "Are you all right?"

She nodded and whispered, "I love you."

His dark eyes flashed. Her message had been received.

"Here's what's going to happen," Thorson said. "We go to the house together. I get the password and transfer funds from the offshore account. When my deposit has cleared, I'll take another ride on the chopper."

"You don't need to drag along Emily or the pilot," Connor said. "I'll be your hostage."

Thorson barked a short, ugly laugh. "Are you trying to negotiate? Don't you understand that I could kill us all with one flick of my thumb?"

"You don't want to die," Connor said. "Not when you're so close to cashing in."

"Okay, the pilot can stay here, but Emily comes with you and me."

Before Connor could object, she spoke up. "I'll do it."

"Good girl," Thorson said. "You two go first. I'll follow."

Climbing down from the chopper, she felt a twinge from her ankle. This much activity wasn't good for the sprain, but she managed to walk fairly well. As they approached the house, she glimpsed a flash of light among the pine trees on the hillside. Was it the reflection of sunlight off the lens of a rifle scope? She suspected there were several cops and deputies hiding in the forest and possibly inside the house.

The front door flung open, and Patricia Riggs stood there with her fists on her hips. She glared at the man

who had once been her fiancé. "You bastard, how could
you do all these terrible things?"

Under his breath, Thorson muttered, "I'd rather face
the SWAT team."

"Step aside," Connor said. "We're coming in."

They rushed into the house, and Patricia closed the
door behind them. In the foyer, Phillip had taken a pro-
prietary position, leaning against the carved-oak banister at the foot of the staircase. He presumed to greet
them like the lord of the castle. *Jerk!* Emily paused and
looked around, taking in her surroundings.

She hadn't been inside this house for over two years,
and her first impression was that Phillip hadn't changed
much of anything. The decor was the same, as was the
arrangement of furniture. He'd left the small Renoir
in the elaborate frame hanging on the back wall of the
foyer. It was one of the first things a guest would see
upon entering—a sun-dappled pastel of a child in a garden. During the good years of her marriage, she used
to think that little girl was her own. Today, the painting failed to charm her. The atmosphere in the house
was totally different.

"You know what I want," Thorson said.

"What about me?" Patricia demanded. "What about
what I want?"

Connor confronted her directly. "This man is wearing a suicide vest. If he lifts his thumb off the kill
switch, we're all dead. I advise you to stay back and
keep quiet."

Moving as quickly as possible, Emily crossed the
front room, circled past the grand piano and stopped

in front of a small desk. Above the desk was *The Note Taker*. "Connor, would you take that painting off the wall?"

"Hey," Phillip said as he stepped forward. "What do you think you're doing?"

"You've been warned to stay quiet. Nobody needs to get hurt."

Connor lifted the painting down and carried it to a glass-topped coffee table. As she gazed down at the simple picture, her heart beat faster. What if she was wrong? Thorson said he wanted to deposit the money before he'd let them go. If she couldn't give him the password, she wasn't sure what he'd do.

"Turn it over," she said to Connor. "I need to see the back side of the canvas."

The notation she'd hoped for was readily visible. Scrawled in Jamison's messy writing was the name of a bank, the password and the account number.

"Good work," Thorson said as he pushed her out of the way and sat on the sofa beside the coffee table. "Everybody, stand back. And don't try anything. I'm going to set down my gun, but I still have the kill switch."

While he sent a text on his phone, she noticed Patricia and Phillip conferring with each other. They were up to something, but Emily didn't care what kind of plot they'd hatched. As soon as this house was sold, the Riggs family would no longer be her problem. She wouldn't miss the luxury, but she loved the artwork. She wandered to the fireplace and looked up at the Remington painting of a mustang herd charging across the plains. Whenever she looked at this vivid picture, she could almost hear the pounding of hooves and the whinny of the horses. Not today. The color seemed muted. The proportions of the central horse were off. The artist never would have made a mistake like that.

Thorson leaned back on the sofa. "My message was sent. Now we wait until I have confirmation."

"I should contact Wellborn," Connor said.

"Not yet." Thorson held up the kill switch to remind him.

They were in more danger than Connor knew. Emily had figured out what was wrong with the house, why it was uncomfortable. Patricia and Phillip were the ones to fear. She looked down, not wanting to betray her suspicions.

In less than ten minutes, Thorson's phone rang. They waited in suspense while he answered and talked. When he disconnected the call, he allowed himself a satisfied grin. "You're looking at a very rich man."

"Deactivate the switch," Connor said.

"With pleasure." Thorson fiddled with the mechanism. He released it. No explosion. "If anything goes south, I can reactivate in a few seconds. For right now, I can't wait to get out of this vest. It's too hot."

He peeled it off, set the explosives aside and rose to his feet.

Phillip aimed his handgun and fired.

Thorson hardly had a chance to look down and see the blood spreading across his muscular chest. The bullet had been lethally accurate—straight through the heart. Dr. Thorson was dead before he hit the floor.

Phillip stared at her. "You figured it out."

"This Remington over the fireplace is a copy. I'm guessing you sold the original."

"Good guess," he said. "Now you know why I couldn't let you into the house. Nobody else noticed, but you're an expert."

"How many others have you sold?"

"Enough to support me in style. I started making substitutions when Jamison was still coming here. He never appreciated the art."

"And you do?"

"I appreciate what it can do for me." Almost casually, Phillip sauntered across the room. "This is working out just the way I wanted. Thorson is out of the way. Now I take care of you two. And I'll use the doctor's gun. Patricia and I will corroborate each other's stories about how Thorson shot both of you. Then I shot him."

"You and Patricia provided alibis for each other before," Emily said, "when you killed Kate."

"That bitch had it coming," he said. "She wanted to blab to the cops."

Thorson hadn't lied to her. He was more of a dupe than a villain. "And you shot at me outside my gallery."

"That was a difficult shot," Phillip said. "Three attempts from a moving vehicle, and I got you in the chest. When you slumped, I thought this was finally over. Damn you, Emily! Why wouldn't you stay dead?"

He reached down to grab Thorson's gun, but Connor was faster. He yanked the weapon into his hands and pointed the barrel in Phillip's direction.

But Phillip hesitated. His plan had been disrupted. She guessed that he didn't want to shoot them with his own weapon because the ballistics would be hard to explain.

Emily took advantage. She grabbed a Navajo wedding vase from the mantle and hurled it at Phillip. The earthenware vase bounced off him and crashed to the floor, but it was enough of a distraction for Connor to charge forward and unload a roundhouse right on Phillip's aristocratic chin. He followed up with three hard gut shots.

Phillip's knees buckled, and he fell to the floor. Connor took his gun and handed it to Emily. "You're a better shot than I am," he said.

"How do you know? You've never seen me take target practice."

"You've got that gunslinger vibe," he said. "Keep an eye on Patricia. I should put in a call to Wellborn."

The phone call was unnecessary. At the sound of Phillip's gunshot, Wellborn and all the other cops who had been lurking at the perimeter of the property converged. They poured through the front door and the patio doors and dashed down the central staircase. While they arrested the Riggs siblings and started all the forensics associated with Thorson's murder, Emily allowed Connor to lead her down the hallway to a library.

He closed the door, holding back the sounds of the investigation coming to a close. And she meandered around the room, staring at the art on the walls. "It breaks my heart to see copies instead of originals."

"We'll take care of it." He pulled her into an embrace

and lightly kissed her lips. "You said something important to me when I saw you on the chopper."

"I did." A wonderful warm sensation spread through her.

"I never had a chance to respond," he said. "I love you, too."

She had a very good feeling about what would happen next. For one thing, people would stop trying to kill her. For another, she had the best of reasons to stay alive.

* * * * *

Look for more books from
USA TODAY *bestselling author Cassie Miles,*
coming in 2019.

And don't miss some of her previous titles:

Mountain Shelter
Mountain Blizzard
Frozen Memories

Available now from Harlequin Intrigue!

INTRIGUE

Available November 20, 2018

#1821 UNDERCOVER CONNECTION
by Heather Graham

FBI agent Jacob Wolff and Miami detective Jasmine Adair are frustrated when they discover they're both undercover to take down the same crime group. After their main informant is killed, can they find a way to work together to stop the ring before anyone else dies?

#1822 FIVE WAYS TO SURRENDER
Mission: Six • by Elle James

Navy SEAL Jake Schuler rescues Alexandria Parker, a teacher, from a group of terrorists in Niger. Will their teamwork be enough to save the other captives?

#1823 BULLETPROOF CHRISTMAS
Crisis: Cattle Barge • by Barb Han

Rory Scott returns to Cattle Barge on business, but his trip turns personal when he sees that Cadence Butler, a woman with whom he had an unforgettable fling, is pregnant. He will do anything to keep Cadence safe, especially since his unborn twins are in danger.

#1824 DELTA FORCE DADDY
Red, White and Built: Pumped Up • by Carol Ericson

Delta Force lieutenant Asher Knight has amnesia after a botched mission. When Paige Sterling claims she's his fiancée, he starts questioning everything around him, including whether the doctors at the rehabilitation center are helping him recover—or keeping him from remembering his past.

#1825 RENEGADE PROTECTOR
by Nico Rosso

Someone will do anything to get Mariana Balducci to sell her family orchard. Ty Morrison, a San Francisco cop and a member of a secret organization known as Frontier Justice, is Mariana's only hope...if she can trust him.

#1826 WYOMING CHRISTMAS RANSOM
Carsons & Delaneys • by Nicole Helm

Coroner Gracie Delaney has never believed Will Cooper's theory that the car accident that killed his wife two years ago was actually a murder. When Will's car is tampered with, causing a near-fatal crash, Gracie must accept that Will may be right. If so, a seasoned killer is now targeting Will.

HICNM1118

Get 4 FREE REWARDS!

We'll send you 2 FREE Books plus 2 FREE Mystery Gifts.

Harlequin® Intrigue books feature heroes and heroines that confront and survive danger while finding themselves irresistibly drawn to one another.

FREE Value Over $20

SPECIAL EXCERPT FROM

H HARLEQUIN®

INTRIGUE

An undercover cop and a deep-cover FBI agent have to team up to take down an organized crime ring on the sultry Miami Beach strip...

Keep reading for a sneak preview of
Undercover Connection,
a thrilling new romantic suspense from
New York Times *bestselling author Heather Graham.*

An absolute melee had begun.

Jasmine helped up a young man, a white-faced rising star in a new television series. He tried to thank her.

"Get out, go—walk quickly," she said.

There were no more gunshots. But would they begin again?

She made her way to Josef Smirnoff, ducking beneath the notice of his distracted bodyguards. She knelt by him as people raced around her. "Josef?" she said, reaching for his shoulder, turning him over.

Blood covered his chest. Covered him. There was no hope for the man; he was already dead, his eyes open in shock. There was blood on her now, blood on the designer gown she'd been wearing, everywhere.

She looked up; Jorge had to be somewhere nearby.

That's when she knew she was about to be attacked herself.

There was a man coming after her, reaching for her.

She rolled quickly, avoiding him once. But as she prepared to fight back, she felt as if she had been taken down by a linebacker. She stared up into the eyes of the shaggy-haired newcomer. Bright blue eyes, startling against his face and dark hair. She felt his hands on her, felt the strength in his hold.

No. She was going to take him down.

She jack-knifed her body, letting him use his own weight against himself, causing him to crash into the floor.

He was obviously surprised; it took him a second—but only a second—to spin himself. He was back on his feet in a hunched position, ready to spring at her.

Where the hell was Jorge?

She feinted, as if she would dive down to the left, dove to the right instead, and caught the man with a hard chop to the abdomen that should have stolen his breath.

He didn't give; she was suddenly tackled again, down on the ground, feeling the full power of the man's strength atop her. She stared up into his eyes, blue eyes, glistening ice at the moment.

She realized the crowd was gone; she could hear the bustle at the doorway, hear the police as they poured in at the entrance.

But right there, at that moment Josef Smirnoff lay dead in an ungodly pool of blood—blood she wore—just feet away.

And there was this man.

And herself.

"Hey!" Thank God, Jorge had found her.

He dove down beside them, as if joining the fight.

But he didn't help Jasmine; he made no move against the man. He lay by Jasmine, as if he'd just been floored himself.

He whispered urgently, "Stop! FBI, meet MDPD. Jasmine, he's undercover. Jacob… Jasmine is a cop. My partner."

The man couldn't have looked more surprised. Then he made a play of socking Jorge, and Jorge lay still.

Jacob stood and dragged Jasmine to her feet. For a long moment he looked into her eyes, and then he wrenched her elbow behind her back.

"Play it out," he said, "nothing else to do."

"Sure," Jasmine told him.

And as he led her out—toward Victor Kozak, who now stood in the front, ready to take charge, Jasmine managed to twist and deliver a hard right to his jaw.

He swirled her around again, staring at her, and rubbing his jaw with his free hand.

"Play it out," she said softly.

Don't miss
Undercover Connection
by New York Times *bestselling author Heather Graham,*
available November 20, 2018, wherever
Harlequin® Intrigue books and ebooks are sold.

www.Harlequin.com